WHAT'S UP WITH JODY BARTON?

Have you ever been hit by a major freakquake?

Hayley Long was born in Ipswich ages ago. She studied English at university in Wales, where she had a very nice time and didn't do much work. After that she spent several years in various places abroad and had a very nice time and didn't do much work then either. Now Hayley is an English teacher and works very hard indeed. She lives in Norwich with a rabbit called Irma and a husband.

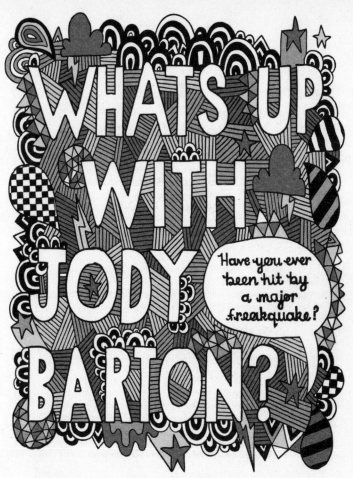

WHATS UP WITH JODY BARTON?

Have you ever been hit by a major freakquake?

Hayley Long

MACMILLAN CHILDREN'S BOOKS

First published 2012 by Macmillan Children's Books
a division of Macmillan Publishers Limited
20 New Wharf Road, London N1 9RR
Basingstoke and Oxford
Associated companies throughout the world
www.panmacmillan.com

ISBN 978-0-330-52302-8

1 3 5 7 9 8 6 4 2

A CIP catalogue record for this book is available from
the British Library.

Printed and bound by CPI Group (UK) Ltd, Croydon CR0 4YY

I don't care whether I am a minx or a sphinx . . .

— *Our Mutual Friend*, Charles Dickens

LIFE CAN BE PRETTY WEIRD SOMETIMES...

It seriously can.

Sometimes, just when you think you're rocking along nicely and minding your own business, life throws you a complete curveball and leaves you feeling totally and utterly freaked-out.

And when that happens the important thing is to stay calm and not do anything stupid.

So far in my life, I've had to cope with three of these curveballs and they've all been thrown at me within the past year. The first came just before the end of Year 10, when Chatty Chong gave me his phone number. Chatty Chong never gives his phone number to anyone. Usually, he doesn't even *speak* to anyone. That's why everyone calls him Chatty Chong. But then, one day, at the end of a maths lesson, he walked over to my desk, dumped his massive Gola bag down on it and said, 'Do you want to pair up with me on this next maths project, yeah?'

And I shrugged my shoulders and said, 'OK then.' Because Chatty Chong is brilliant at maths. He's even better at it than I am and I got 96% in my last test. And Mrs Hamood, my maths teacher, said I would have got top marks if I'd spent more time on improper fractions and less time doodling in the answer book.

Chatty Chong sort of smiled and said, 'I'll give you my number so we can talk about maths on the phone, yeah?'

And I shrugged my shoulders and said, 'OK then.'

So he unzipped his bag, took out his pencil tin and scribbled down his phone number on a piece of graph paper. And then he pushed the paper towards me, sort of smiled again and said, 'See you tomorrow, yeah?' And without another word to anyone he picked up his Gola bag and walked out of the classroom.

But here's the really weird bit.

When I looked down at that piece of paper, my heart nearly stopped. Chatty Chong's phone number was almost exactly the same as mine. Apart from one single digit. All the other digits matched completely. They were even in the same order! When I saw this, it flipped me out so much that, at first, I thought it must have been some sort of weird joke. And then, because I really *couldn't* believe it and needed to check, I took my phone out of my bag and punched in Chatty's number.

After half a ring, I heard Chatty say, 'Yeah?'

I said, 'It's me already. I wanted to tell you that our phone numbers are practically identical. Apart from one digit.'

Chatty Chong went silent on the line for a few seconds and, even though there was loads of background noise from the corridor, I swear to God I could hear his brain ticking over. Then he said, 'You're joking with me, yeah?'

And I said, 'No. I'm deadly serious.'

Chatty Chong whistled loudly down the phone.

I said, 'OI,' and ripped the phone away from my ear. Then, after a second or two, I put it back and said, 'ARE YOU TRYING TO TRASH MY EARDRUM OR WHAT?'

Chatty Chong said, 'Sorry.' And, to be fair, he did sound genuinely apologetic. Then he said, 'It's just that the probability of that happening is one in a *billion*. And that's without even counting the zero at the beginning. Otherwise, it would have been one in *ten* billion. But it's still a big coincidence, yeah?' And then the line went dead and I realized he'd ended the call. Like I said before, Chatty Chong is brilliant at maths. He's a bit bad at chatting though.

The second freaky curveball got chucked at me just after that while I was on holiday in Spain. We'd only been there a few days when my sister started getting really intense stomach pains. To begin with, we all just laughed at her for pigging out on paella. My sister does tend to exaggerate rather a lot and she *had* queued up for third helpings of the main course the night before. But pretty soon I realized she was in proper crippling agony and I told my parents she needed to see a doctor fast. Then, after she'd seen a doctor, we realized she needed an emergency operation to have her appendix removed. The entire experience was freaky and horrible because I felt about as much use as a chocolate teapot. I don't speak a word of Spanish so I couldn't even organize a top-up for her phone. Even though she gets on my nerves, we're as close as two freckles and seeing her look so manky and ill was horrible. To make matters worse, neither of us had any phone credit for almost three weeks. I never want to go through an experience like that ever again.

But the most head-spinning moment of my entire life happened in February, a few weeks before my birthday. And although what I'm about to tell you may seem a helluva lot less dramatic than my sister nearly popping her clogs in a Spanish hospital it still felt massively dramatic to me. In fact, it felt as if I'd been hit by a major freakquake of a magnitude of 8.35 – and, for your information, that's as powerful as the blast from a nuclear bomb! So I'm talking about one seriously intense curveball.

Or, to put it more precisely . . .

I'm talking about the very first time I looked over and saw Liam Mackie's face.

And although I managed to stay calm and didn't do anything stupid on that *particular* occasion it was really only a matter of time before I *would*. But I'll come to all of that later.

Because there's a lot to tell you and I need to start at the beginning.

And in the beginning I was in the cafe and The Doors were playing at top volume. I should just explain that I love The Doors. They're my favourite band. And Jim Morrison, their lead singer, is my favourite singer.

I drew this picture of him in my maths book.

Jim
Morrison
(1943-1971)

Sadly, pictures and posters are pretty much all that's left because he died the exact same year that both my parents were born. This means that he never owned an Xbox, never planted his feet into a fresh pair of K-Swiss trainers and didn't even know what a status update was. But none of that matters to me.

I still think he's amazing.

And, while I'm on the subject, River Phoenix was amazing too.

River was an American actor and he died even younger than Jim did. In my opinion, River and Jim are two of the most incredible people who have ever existed. I've got pictures of both of them on my bedroom walls and I sit and look at them a lot. And quite frankly, until I saw Liam Mackie, I was never remotely interested in looking at anybody else.

But I was telling you about The Doors. My favourite track of all is a song called 'Light My Fire'. When it begins, it sounds just like any other cheery pop song, but pretty quickly it becomes clear that things aren't always what they seem. Because, instead of being a few minutes long like most songs, this one just keeps on going and going. And all the time it's getting louder and louder and faster and faster, and Jim just keeps on singing in this really intense and dark and hypnotic way for almost eight minutes. I get goose bumps every time I hear it. But the reason I'm talking about all this now is because it was this exact song that was playing in the cafe when I first looked at Liam Mackie. If I believed in superstitious spooky stuff, I'd say that Jim Morrison was trying to tell me something.

And when I close my eyes I can take myself right back to that very second. The Doors are turned up as loud as they'll go and Liam Mackie is sitting on his own at a table by the window. In front of him is an untouched strawberry and banana smoothie. He has one foot resting on the empty chair opposite him and the other is tapping against the floor tiles to the beat of 'Light My Fire'. His head is gently nodding along too. It's the most effortlessly cool hipster head bop I've ever seen. And even from the other side of the cafe I can see that this boy is incredibly good-looking. I'd have to be blind not to see it. And it's almost like I'm looking at River Phoenix. Only this time I'm not a saddo staring at a poster on my bedroom wall – I'm a saddo in an embarrassing orange apron staring at an actual proper person.

But only for a second.

Because as soon as I realize that I'm staring at him I quickly look down and frown at the floor.

But it's too late. Something has sparked inside me. It actually feels like there's a firework trapped in my body. Or as if I've been struck by forked lightning or something. And, suddenly, I know that something utterly weird has happened. And it's the kind of weird thing that I thought only ever happens in drippy books or romantic movies. I never thought it would ever happen to me. Not like this anyway. Never like this.

In the space of a single second, I've fallen hopelessly and helplessly and head-over-hi-tops in love with the boy who looks like River Phoenix.

And then my sister nudges my arm, nods her head in his direction and says, 'See that fit guy over there? I totally intend to go out with him.'

Me and my sister are twins. She's Jolene and I'm Jody. We've both got brown hair, we're both left-handed and we both have these weirdly long little toes that make us look like long-toed mutants. Also, we've both got hazel eyes that change colour depending on what we're wearing and we both get these funny dents in our cheeks when we laugh. But apart from that I'd say we're fairly different.

Well, actually, we're a lot different.

In fact, we're so totally and utterly and entirely different that we weren't even born on the same day. *That's* how different we are.

Jolene was born a few minutes before midnight at the end of one day and I flumped out fourteen minutes later at the start of the next. And straight away, before the ink had even dried on my birth certificate, I learned the importance of turning up to things on time. And now I'm never late. Not to school. Not to the cafe. Not to anything. Because, sometimes, rocking up fourteen minutes late can be a massively big deal. And it can also mean that you miss out on certain things.

Like birthdays.

I've only properly genuinely had four birthdays in my entire life – and I'm sixteen years old. My fourteen-minutes-faster twin has had all sixteen of hers. The other week, my parents took us out to the London Dungeon and then on to Pizza Shack to celebrate the fact that Jolene was officially sixteen and I was officially four. But when all the stuff in this story was happening she was still fifteen and I was still three.

Confused?

So are most people. But, actually, it's quite simple. Jolene was born on the twenty-eight of February and I was born, fourteen minutes later, at 12:08 a.m. on the morning of the twenty-ninth.

Which means I was born on a leap day.

Which means I am officially what is known as a leapling!

Now being a twin isn't such a massively unusual thing. The last I heard, the probability was about 1 in 32. This means that there should roughly be one twin in almost every class in my school.

But being a leapling like me *is* unusual. You won't find one of us in every classroom. You won't even find one of us in every school. Because the likelihood of being born on the twenty-ninth of February is only 1 in 1,461. And, even though that's nowhere near as random as finding out that you've got the exact same phone number – except for one single digit – as your maths-project partner, it's still pretty damn rare, I reckon. And when you think about it I'm probably the rarest leapling of the lot. Because, if you did a survey to find out how many leaplings have a twin born on a totally different day, I bet anything you like that the answer would be one. Me. Mrs Hamood once told me I was a mathematical curiosity. I went red when she said this. I was pleased though.

But, maths compliments aside, being a leapling mostly sucks. Seventy-five per cent of the time, I'm forced to share Jolene's birthday on the twenty-eighth and, although she's usually very cool about this, we both know that it's her special day much more than it is mine. Take when we were ten, for instance. My mum and dad had a big party for us in the cafe and we were allowed to choose a film for all our friends to watch. I wanted to see *Ice Age 2 – The Meltdown* and Jolene wanted to see *Pirates of the Caribbean – Dead Man's Chest*. We ended up with my choice because Jolene got nasty and said, 'Whose birthday is it, actually, anyway?'

My dad overheard her and said, 'Right, that's it. You're watching the ice thing.'

But in the end I didn't enjoy a single second of that film. I was too busy feeling bad about gate-crashing Jolene's party.

And then there are the conversations like the one I had

once with Chatty Chong. He asked me when I was sixteen and I said, 'End of February.'

And he said, 'What day?'

And I said, 'The twenty-ninth.'

And Chatty said, 'No way, yeah?'

And I said, 'Way yeah!'

And Chatty whistled in amazement and said, 'So you're actually only three, innit!' And then he went all quiet and looked a bit freaked out.

So, anyway, Jolene and I are totally different. But, to be honest, most twins are. Even the ones who look like they've been photocopied. Check them out closely and you'll see what I'm saying. There's always one who's fractionally taller, slightly smarter and a bit better-looking than the other.

I'd love to say that in our case that person is me. But I can't. Because it would be plain wrong.

And there's no way I'm going to say it's Jolene. Because that would be plain wrong too.

The truth is that it's pointless even going down that route. We're polar opposites. If I was explaining all this to Chatty Chong or to Mrs Hamood, I'd just draw a diagram of a very big circle and place me and Jolene at either end of its diameter. Like this:

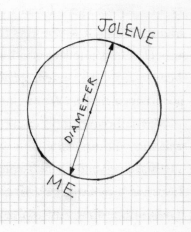

But most people don't think in maths diagrams so I'll try to explain myself a bit more clearly in words.

Jolene is a complete jabber-jaws and I'm fairly quiet.

Jolene is always late to things and I'm always on time.

Jolene spends forty minutes in the bathroom every morning and I don't.

Jolene does our geography, RE and German homework and I do our art, music and maths. (We take our own individual chances on all the other stuff.)

Jolene thinks Chatty Chong is a *Nerdasaurus-rex* whereas I think he's all right.

Jolene loves listening to Beyoncé and The Black-Eyed Peas and I only like The Doors.

Jolene walks stupidly slowly and I walk stupidly fast.

So really we're about as twinny as pork and peas. But that doesn't mean that we don't get along because we definitely do. And, even though we wind each other up and call each other names and steal each other's stuff and eat each other's Easter eggs, I really love my twin sister. And she loves me too. I know this for a fact because most of the time I've got a pretty good idea of what's going on inside her head. I suppose it's called my *twi*ntuition. Whenever she's happy or sad or excited or bored, I usually know about it before she even tells me. For some weird reason though, this twintuition only ever travels in one direction. I'm really good at guessing what's going on in Jolene's head, but she's hopeless at working out what's going on in mine. I think she knows it's mostly stuff connected with my maths GCSE and she's stopped taking an interest.

Even so, we're close. How could we not be? She's my fourteen-minutes-faster sister and we've been laughing our heads off over private jokes and hanging around together since before we were even born. But I've got to admit that, every now and again, there are odd moments when I catch myself thinking about how much easier it might be if I wasn't one half of twins. I don't think this often. Just on random occasions. And one of those random occasions was that freaky moment in the cafe when we both got butterflies over the exact same person.

WELCOME TO MY WORLD

WILLESDEN GREEN

Me and Jolene live in a maisonette above a cafe. The cafe is called Chunky's Diner and the owner – Chunky Barton – just happens to be our dad. When I'm not at school or in my bedroom or hanging out at Brent Cross Shopping Centre, I'm almost always helping my dad by doing a bit of washing up or wiping a few tables or pressing a few buttons on the microwave. Usually, Jolene is there helping out too. And, in return, he gives us a big fat wodge of cash to spend.

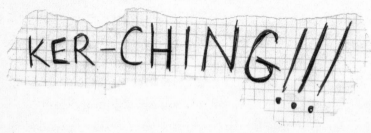

KER-CHING!!!

It's a really top deal because I don't mind the work. I don't even mind that my dad makes us wear hideous bright orange T-shirts and matching aprons that have got ASK ME ABOUT OUR CHAMPION CHUNKY BREAKFAST printed on them. It's still way better than delivering leaflets or holding a big sign with an arrow on it that says GOLF SALE. And, to be honest, there isn't actually ever that much to do because we've only got about ten regular customers and they never come in all at once. Occasionally, some random boring person will walk in and ask for a sausage roll or a bacon sandwich and then my dad will get very excited and say:

'New customer?'

And the random boring person usually smiles and nods and mumbles something about just passing by or being lost and my dad smiles back and says, 'Do me a favour, pal. If you like what we do here, tell everyone. And if you don't like what we do tell the wife.'

Then they both laugh as if my dad has just said something seriously witty — even though he quite blatantly hasn't.

And a little while later, my dad turns to Jolene and me and says, 'I bet you anything in the world that our new customer rode all the way here on the Chunky Bus.' Then he winks — just like he's the wisest person in the whole of Willesden — and starts happily singing as he fries his onions. And the song he's always singing goes like this: 'And it burns . . . burns . . . burns . . . the ring of fire.' It's an ancient song by a spooky old American cowboy called Johnny Cash.

The Chunky Bus is a private joke. What my dad is

actually referring to is the number 98, which runs between Holborn and Willesden Green. It travels right through the heart of London and then it heads up past Marble Arch and on through Maida Vale and straight through Kilburn and it keeps on going until it eventually reaches a bus stop directly outside our cafe on Willesden High Road. And this is where everyone always gets off. Sometimes one or two of them will come into our cafe. After that, the number 98 carries on for just another hundred metres or so as far as the Willesden bus depot and, once it's there, it turns right round and heads straight back to the West End. My dad reckons this is specifically so it can scoop up another load of tourists who can't wait to swap the fancy restaurants and the glazzamatazz of central London for a genuine Champion Chunky Breakfast in Chunky's Diner. My dad is a seriously funny man sometimes.

Then there's my mum. She can be quite funny too when she wants to be. Her name is Angie Barton. Like me and Jolene, she has brown hair and hazel eyes and she's actually still really attractive even though she's forty, wears a lot of leopard print and fiddles with her hair too much. Whenever she comes up to our school for open evenings, she easily out-glams all the other mums. They all look like Iggy Pop compared to her. I have to say, though, that sometimes her sense of humour is a bit random. I'll give you an example: if it had been left to her, our cafe would now be called Angie's Tasty Baps. Whichever way you look at it, this is even worse than naming it Chunky's Diner. Luckily, it was a family decision and the rest of us ganged together and overruled her on this occasion.

But that's my mum. She's always been a loose cannon when it comes to naming things. She was the one who dished out the names for me and Jolene, and she nearly made a mess of that too.

'I wanted to give you names that reflect my love of music,' she's said to us a million times.

'Fine,' Jolene has snapped – a million times – back at her. 'So why couldn't you have called me Britney or Kylie or Mariah or Fergie? Any of those would have been cool. But why the heck *Jolene*? I'm the only Jolene in my entire school. It makes me feel like a freak.'

That's another difference between Jolene and me. She's a total drama queen. I'm totally not.

And, without fail, my mum always says, '*Fergie?* Why on earth would I name you after that strumpet? She's brought nothing but shame upon the good name of our royal family.' Then she starts fiddling furiously with one of her honey-coloured hair extensions and says, 'You know full well why I called you Jolene! It's the title of my most favourite song *ever*. And it's a beautiful song and Jolene is a beautiful name so stop breaking my heart, you ungrateful little madam, and thank your lucky stars I didn't call you Backwoods Barbie.'

This is my mum's idea of a private joke. Unfortunately, it's *such* a private joke that she's the only one of us who actually gets it.

And then – and this is where the story gets really disturbing – my mum turns to me and says, 'I wanted to call *you* Dolly – after the beautiful woman who sang that beautiful song.' And she begins to twiddle a hair extension round her little finger and puts her head on one side and laughs. And all the time she's laughing she's looking at me with big round emotional eyes and I'm never quite sure what to do with myself.

My mum is talking about an American country music singer who has very big hair and very big bazookas and who's called Dolly Parton.

If my mum *had* gone ahead with her genius plan, I'd now be called . . .

Dolly Barton.

So I reckon that's why I wasn't in any hurry to be born, and hung on inside for those extra fourteen minutes. I was just giving my mum plenty of time to change her mind.

'I'm glad you didn't call me that,' I always say. 'I'd have been a total joke.'

But my mum just carries on looking at me with this weird faraway look on her face and says, 'It's a shame, Jody. I'd *absolutely* set my heart on calling you Dolly. Jolene and Dolly. My very own country-music twincesses. I had it all planned out and *nothing* was going to change my mind. But then you popped out and it was obvious that you weren't a Dolly!'

So, anyway, she eventually decided to call me Jody – for no better reason than that it worked well in a pair with Jolene. And, even though it's not what *I'd* have chosen, I'm cool with it. After hearing that horror story, who wouldn't be?

So we all live up above Chunky's Diner. Mum, Dad, Jolene and me. Personally, I love it. My bedroom is at the very top of the house and I can look down on all the cars and vans and double-decker buses, and if I press my face right up against the glass of my window I can even see the big white arch of Wembley peeping over the rooftops. I don't like football, but I like Wembley. And I like that arch. I don't know why but it makes me happy whenever I see it. Maybe because it looks like a big weird rainbow hanging over north-west London. Or like the handle on a giant's shopping basket.

And, even though it's not the poshest place in the world, I like Willesden High Road too. It's got practically everything I need. Like a library and a supermarket and a cake shop and a tube station. It's also got a lot of other stuff I don't need. Like sixteen hairdressers and four tanning salons and a really random shop that sells nothing but old front doors and fireplaces. But at least it means that there's always plenty happening on our street. And there are always plenty of weird and way-out people walking around on the other side of our big cafe window. I swear to God I saw Justin Bieber once. And Nelson Mandela. And Lady Gaga. She was wrapped up in a tartan blanket and riding along on a mobility scooter.

I read on the internet that 7,172,091 people live in London. That's more than seven million people. They all wander down Willesden High Road at some point. Somebody interesting was bound to push open our cafe door sooner or later. Then, one rainy Sunday afternoon in early February, somebody interesting did.

THE MEANING OF BEAUTIFUL

Jolene saw him first. Of course she did. She's fourteen minutes ahead of me in absolutely everything. She watched him jump down from the Chunky Bus, flick the hair out of his eyes with a sudden sideways jerk of the head and then lean against our window and chat for a bit on his mobile phone.

My dad has a real issue with people doing this. For some reason, he reckons it's bad for business. He even went through this embarrassing phase of charging outside and saying, 'What do you think this is? A Public Leaning Post?' One day he made the mistake of saying it to Natalie Snell and her mum. Natalie Snell is the hardest girl in my school and her mum is even harder. My dad said, 'What do you think this is, ladies? A Public Leaning Post?'

And Natalie Snell's mum looked him up and down, blew a massive bubble in her pink bubblegum and said, 'Nah, mate. From where I'm standing it looks like a fat bloke with an attitude problem.'

So my dad doesn't tend to hassle people any more. He usually just lets them lean. He's not happy about it though.

But that Sunday afternoon my dad wasn't around to get upset. He'd popped out to buy 400 turkey twizzlers from Frosty Frank. My mum wasn't around either. She'd nipped down to The Talon Salon to have her nails sharpened. So neither of them saw the boy leaning against our window. And neither did they see him put his phone away, push his hands into his pockets and bump open the door of our cafe with his shoulder.

Or that's how Jolene tells it anyway. She also says it was the hottest head-turning Hollywood entrance she's ever seen in her entire life. Considering that we're in Willesden Green and nearly all our customers are over seventy, there's probably a lot of truth in that.

But I wouldn't know. I was busy scraping food off plates and into the bin. As far as I was concerned, whoever had walked in was just another random boring customer.

I heard the Random Boring Customer say, 'Strawberry and banana smoothie, please. Just fruit. No yoghurt, OK?'

And then I heard my sister Jolene say, 'It's your smoothie – have it how you like. Anything else?'

And the RBC said, 'Nah, just that thanks.'

And then I heard the sound of his strawberries and

bananas being whizzed together in the blender and a minute or so later I heard Jolene say, 'That'll be one seventy-five then, please.'

He said, 'Cheers.'

She said, 'Ta.'

Coins clinked. The drawer of the cash register clunked. And somewhere a chair scraped against the tiles as the Random Boring Customer pulled it away from a table and sat down.

Big fat deal.

So I carried on scraping plates, and then, when that was done, I moved over to the sink and switched my attention to the massive stack of washing up. I should just explain that we don't have a separate kitchen in our cafe. Our entire catering operation depends on nothing more than a hot-plate, a microwave and a sink behind the counter. Dad says separate kitchens create an unfriendly barrier between the caterer and the customer. And, anyway, we don't have the space for one. I should also explain that it's always me who does the washing up. Jolene won't do it because she reckons it wrecks her nail transfers. I don't have any transfers on my nails so I'm not bothered.

I turned both taps on full and watched as a mutant blob of soapy foam began to grow inside the sink.

'Jody?'

At first I didn't hear. The water was sploshing into the sink with such force that my ears thought they were in Niagara.

'Jody!'

I turned off one of the taps and looked round. And then I jumped. Jolene was right behind me. Even though she's my twin and we're very close, she was invading my personal body space. I took a step backwards.

'I need to tell you something,' she whispered. It was a loud whisper, but it was still definitely a whisper. Her hands had gone into mime overdrive and her mouth was working way too hard. I quickly turned off the other tap and took a step forward.

'What?' I said. I was loud-whispering too. I don't know why. A very quick glance past her shoulder told me that there was hardly anyone around to ear-jack our conversation anyway. The cafe was quieter than Mrs Hamood's Monday Maths Club. Just the Random Boring Customer sitting in the corner and Whispering Bob Harris who comes in every single day.

Whispering Bob Harris isn't his real name. Until very recently, we didn't actually know what his real name was. My dad tried to ask him once but WBH just put his hand behind his ear and bellowed, 'Speak up, son. I can't hear you.' And then Jolene *also* tried to ask him and WBH said the *same* thing:

'Speak up, son, I can't hear you.'

I'd laughed so hard I nearly collapsed but Jolene was mortified and kept asking us if she looked like a bloke.

Then we realized that WBH says this to everyone. He'd probably even say it to Dolly Parton given half a chance. He still needed a name though, and for some random reason my dad decided to call him Whispering Bob Harris.

The long and the short of it is that WBH is older than God and as deaf as a doorknob.

So I really didn't need to whisper.

But, just to be safe, I switched on our stereo and turned the volume up as loud as it would go. The song that came blaring out was my all-time favourite. 'Light My Fire'.

'You'll never guess what,' said Jolene, half-shout, half-whisper. She had a soppy grin on her face and her cheeks had gone a bit pink. I smiled to myself. This usually means that she's fallen in love.

'You've fallen in love,' I said.

Jolene looked shocked. And then she shook her head in amazement and said, 'OMG! Is it that obvious! How the heck can you tell?'

I almost laughed out loud. Unlike me, Jolene is *always* falling in love. I reckon she tells me about it at least once a fortnight. And then, just after that, she tells me she's got a new boyfriend and then, just after that, she tells me she's dumped him.

I didn't LOL though because I'm not really the LOL type. And, anyway, it's as tight as a teabag to laugh at people when they're spilling the beans on a sensitive personal issue. So instead I just smiled again and squeezed a load more washing-up liquid into the sink.

Jolene stuck her bottom lip out and said, 'What's so funny?'

'Nothing,' I said, and blew some foam off my face.

'Yes there is,' said Jolene. 'You're laughing at me.'

'I'm not laughing at you,' I said. 'I'm smiling to myself. There's a big difference.'

Jolene frowned. 'Yeah, whatever . . . I'm being serious though, Jode! Don't look now but there's this boy sitting in the window and he's the fittest thing I've ever seen in my life. I love him. Go over to the counter and pretend to be doing something so you can get a proper look – you can see his face from there.'

I couldn't be bothered. I've seen Jolene's dream boyfriends before and they always look like members of JLS.

I picked up a dirty plate and very, very slowly I began to wash it. Out of the corner of my eye, I could see that Jolene's face was looking as if it might pop with impatience. For some reason, this made me smile again and it also made my hands move even slower. To be fair though, that plate had a lot of dried-up egg and tomato sauce stuck to it.

Jolene's face almost twitched off her head. 'What the heck are you doing? Put the plate down and stop being a weirdo! This is important! I need you to look at him now. Quick! He could get up and walk out of my life at any second.'

I dumped the plate back into the foamy water and frowned. 'Quit calling me a weirdo!' And then I said, 'I'm only trying to get these dishes done. It's what Dad pays me to do, remember?'

Jolene sighed and folded her arms. And then she chewed

her thumbnail. And then she said, 'Soz.'

I ignored her.

Jolene said, 'Sozza bozza, Jody Wody.' Her voice had gone a bit high and whiney.

I blew some more foam off my face and started washing up again.

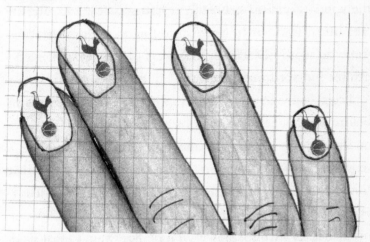

Jolene stood there for a few more seconds, just chewing her nails. It's a very pointless habit considering she takes so much time and trouble over them. On each nail, she happened to have a transfer of the Tottenham Hotspur club badge and all the tooth contact was making some of those cockerels look a bit manky. Jolene is a massive Spurs fan. All my family are except for me. It's nothing personal I've got against Spurs. I just don't like football.

Jolene took her nails out of her mouth and said, 'Soz and chips.' One of her feet had begun to tap against the tiled floor.

'Whatever,' I said. And then I started counting slowly in my head. I got as far as three.

'Look, Jode, I'm proper sorry, yeah?' Jolene said really quickly in a really loud whisper. 'I honestly didn't mean to call you a weirdo. It just came out wrong. The thing is – I'm under A LOT OF EMOTIONAL PRESSURE right now because I genuinely believe that THE LOVE OF MY LIFE is . . . right now . . . sitting in the corner of our cafe and I NEED TO FIND OUT WHO HE IS. And I realize . . . yeah . . . that you don't understand because you're only interested in your maths project and your weird music and stuff . . . and I know you're not remotely interested in having any kind of romantic experience until you're at least a hundred and five . . . but I *AM* INTERESTED and *I'M BEGGING YOU* TO HELP ME FIND OUT WHO THIS BUFF BOY IS. PLEEEEASE!'

She wasn't whispering any more. She wasn't even loud-whispering. She was just being loud. Even with The Doors blaring out of our speakers, it's a wonder Buff Boy didn't hear every single word.

'Call that an apology?' I muttered. And then I picked up a wet tea towel and flicked it at her head. 'More like a *non*pology.' I was quite offended actually. It probably didn't show though because I don't tend to get over-emotional like Jolene does – but she'd hit a raw nerve all the same. So I'm fussy. So what? I've never been the sort who drones on and on about love. That's for other people – not me. And, anyway, Jolene goes on enough random dates for both of us. In fact, she's a serial dater.

Jolene shrugged. 'Just saying.' And then she must have remembered how desperate she was because she looped her arm through mine and started being extra nice. 'Please, Jody. *Please* just come away from the sink just for one second and tell me if you know him. And then *I'll* finish the washing up *and* mop the floor *and* clean the loo and you can do nothing till Dad comes back. Absolutely nothing at all.'

And, even though she'd called me a weirdo and made me sound as exciting as a fridge magnet, this still seemed like a WIN.

'OK,' I said. 'OK. But I'm hardly likely to know him if you don't, am I?' And I threw the tea towel down on the work surface and walked forward to the counter.

'Him over there,' whispered Jolene, and nodded her head towards the corner. She needn't really have bothered. I'd already worked out that it wasn't Whispering Bob Harris she was lusting after. But I followed her gaze anyway. And then I shifted a few steps sideways so that I could get a better look.

And that was when I first properly saw him and it felt just as if I was being struck by lightning.

He wasn't Jolene's usual type at all. Not only did he look nothing like Aston Merrygold, Oritsé Williams, Marvin Humes or J. B. Gill, he actually looked nothing like *any* member of *any* boy band *any*where. He did remind me of someone though.

'It's River Phoenix,' I whispered in disbelief.

The boy in the corner looked just like my favourite gone-but-never-forgotten film star. And, even though I really didn't want to agree with her, I had to admit that Jolene was absolutely spot on. He *was* buff.

Is buff.

Always will be buff.

And nom and peng and fit and hench and all those other words that the girls at school bandy about when they're really just trying to say beautiful.

Or maybe, after all, the word *beautiful* means something entirely different.

In fact, the more I think about it, the more complicated the word *beautiful* becomes.

So I suppose the only thing I can do is try to explain what it meant to *me* at that particular moment. And what it meant was pretty much this:

Imagine a boy with light brown hair that is messy and overgrown, but which somehow manages to look absolutely perfect anyway. His hair falls naturally around his face and you can see immediately that no wax or gel or straightening contraptions have ever touched a single strand of it. His hair just looks good anyway. Hat-head is something that he doesn't have to worry about.

And his face is not too round and not too ratty and not too scowly and not too spotty – it's just a perfect picture of mathematical symmetry. With respect to the y-axis anyway.

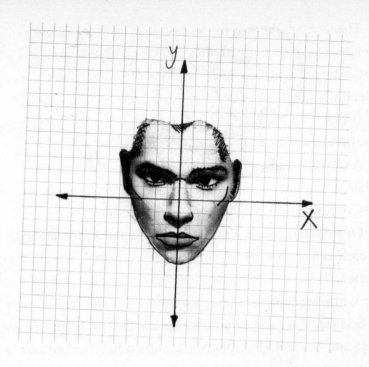

Then there are his clothes. They give him a style all of his own. There isn't a trendy label or a designer logo or a bling-tastic price tag on him. Because this boy is way too cool for fashion. He's quite blatantly cooler than a polar bear's toes. His coat is a moss-green parka with a big furry hood and it has a stripy Irish flag sewn on to the right sleeve. On the left sleeve, in big black chunky marker pen, there's a weird squiggle. At first you can't tell what it is, but, later, when you look again, you see it's a hand-drawn badge for Queen's Park Rangers Football Club.

To be honest, even if you don't like football, you instantly start to feel yourself becoming ever so slightly interested in QPR.

The bottoms of this boy's jeans are fraying where they've dragged on the ground, and on his feet he wears scruffy plimsolls which probably used to be white but are now a dirty grey. Most people would look skanky in an outfit like that. But not him. Not River Phoenix Boy. Even those plimsolls look great on him.

I noticed all this in the space of one single second. It was like time slowed down and my brain whizzed up to warp speed. And all the while that my eyes were drinking in these amazing details my ears were drinking in the sound of The Doors as Jim Morrison shouted out the words to "Light My Fire",' through the cheap fuzzy speakers of the cafe.

It was almost as if River Phoenix and Jim Morrison had been put on this earth specifically to add extra meaning to this one single second in my life.

Mrs Hamood likes to tell my class that mathematics is about a lot more than adding a few numbers together. She reckons it's about everything. Because not only does it help us to manage money, tell the time, bake cakes, make music and understand art – it also allows us to make sense of our entire lives.

But usually it's only me and Chatty Chong who are listening. Everyone else is either fiddling with a phone underneath the desk or using the numbers on their scientific calculators to spell out something side-splittingly hilarious.

Even though I usually agree with Mrs Hamood, I now know that she is wrong. Maths doesn't provide the answer for everything. Some things in life are completely beyond any logical explanation. And for one strange but completely wonderful moment, I looked at the random boy in the corner and the only thing I understood was that I loved him.

And that's when my super-confident serial-dating fourteen-minutes-faster sister nudged my arm and said, 'See that fit guy there? I totally intend to go out with him.'

And suddenly everything about my life seemed seriously complicated.

AN AMAZING LITTLE MIRACLE

'You can't,' I whispered in a panic. 'Not *him*!'

Jolene frowned. 'Why? Do you know him?'

'No,' I said. Which was true.

'So why the heck shouldn't I go after him?' said Jolene.

'Because . . .' I began, 'because . . .' But then I hesitated. I had to. I'd run out of words. And, besides that, I was suddenly experiencing a few other technical glitches – my mouth had gone dry, my armpits were prickling and my brain felt as if it had just been pulled out at the plug. I thumped the side of my head with the palm of my hand in a lame attempt to get it working again.

Jolene's frown deepened. 'You're acting *seriously* weird! What's up with you?'

'Nothing,' I whispered. Which was a lie.

Jolene looked unconvinced.

'I'm fine,' I added quickly. *Too* quickly probably. If my sister had even the tiniest drop of twintuition, she'd have sussed immediately that I wasn't fine. I was excited and dizzy and thunderstruck and feeling weird and covered in goose pimples and slightly sick and also a bit oddly and madly happy – but, hand on heart, I can't seriously say I was fine. To be honest, I was mostly totally freaked out.

'Right,' said Jolene, folding her arms. 'So what's wrong with him?'

I searched through my head and tried to think of something to say – but it was really hard because I was still freaked out. In the end, I just looked down at my hi-tops and said, 'I've got this really weird feeling about him, that's all.' And then I clamped my jaw shut.

'*What?*' I could tell from her big frown that Jolene was getting more and more exasperated. For a moment her eyes left mine and she glanced anxiously over to the corner – no doubt to check that River Phoenix Boy was still sitting safely in his seat. And, even though I was desperate to glance over too, I didn't.

I couldn't.

I was too terrified.

None of our customers had ever given me goose pimples before.

So, instead, I kept my eyes fixed firmly on Jolene and I saw her face relax a little. Clearly River Phoenix Boy was going nowhere fast. This made me relax slightly too. But only very slightly. Because half a second later Jolene's eyes flicked straight back to mine and stayed there. And then she folded her arms even tighter and said, 'What *sort* of weird feeling?'

'I dunno,' I said. I began to bite my thumbnail. This only ever happens when I'm anxious. It's not a big deal or anything because I haven't got stupid transfers all over my nails. Without moving my hand away from my mouth, I muttered, 'He looks like an idiot, that's all.'

Jolene's mouth dropped open in shock. 'You seriously think that?'

'Uh-huh,' I said, and nodded. One hand was still at my mouth and the other was in the pocket of my orange apron to hide my crossed fingers. Normally, I don't lie to Jolene. Not this much, anyway. After all, what's the point of spinning a story to someone you've known since you were half-egg/half-tadpole?

But then again, what's the point of telling the truth when it's going to cause so much trouble?

'He looks like a dork,' I said firmly. For a second I almost believed myself. I definitely wanted to.

Jolene's amazement deepened and her mouth widened. But then she pulled her face back together, shrugged her shoulders and smiled. A little bubble of relief burst inside me.

'Whatever,' she said. That's your opinion and you're entitled to it. Just like I'm entitled to mine. And *I* think he's a totally bufferlicious buffercake and I'm going over

to introduce myself whether *you* think he's a dork or not.'
And then she stuck her tongue out at me.

My relief evaporated. This wasn't the result I'd been hoping for. Normally Jolene doesn't go within a fifteen-mile radius of any guy who's been dissed with the dork tag. Clearly my opinion on these matters didn't count though.

Jolene winked at me and whispered, 'Watch this. I'm about to get myself an A★ in GCSE flirting.'

I panicked. 'What are you gonna do?'

'See if he wants a free top-up on his smoothie.'

'Dad wouldn't like that,' I said. 'You're damaging his profits.'

My sister rolled her eyes. 'Oh, lighten up, Jode. It's just a bit of flipping fruit!'

I couldn't argue with this so I just chewed my thumbnail and watched as Jolene untied the cords of her horrible orange apron and slipped it off. Then she took a couple of paper serviettes out of a box on the counter, scrunched them into two tight balls and quickly poked them down the front of her top.

I smiled then. I couldn't stop myself. Jolene is so utterly flat-chested that you could put a heat-resistant vest on her and use her as an ironing board. Even I'm not as flat as her.

Jolene opened the fridge and took out a banana and some strawberries. To be fair to her, she remembered not to bother with any yoghurt. Then she paused for a second and said, 'What's this music? It's horrible.'

'It's The Doors,' I snapped. 'You should know that by

now – seeing as how they're my favourite band.'

'Yeah, well, they're crap,' said Jolene. 'I'm putting the radio on instead.'

She turned round and reached up to where our dodgy old stereo is fixed to the wall. Quickly, I turned too and risked a glance at the boy in the corner. His head was still bopping along to The Doors and so were his scruffy white plimsolls. Obviously, we were into the same sort of sounds.

What else might we have in common?

I felt my heart sink. It wasn't a question I could answer. Not now. Not ever. Not me.

I picked up a damp cloth and slowly began to wipe the counter.

Abruptly, Jim Morrison stopped singing and some random DJ from some random radio station started rambling on randomly about nothing. Out of the corner of my eye, I noticed that the mystery boy's feet had stopped bopping. Jolene returned to the counter, threw her strawberries and half a banana into the blender, whizzed them up and then poured the mixture into a jug. And then she giggled and whispered, 'Watch and learn, Jody. Watch and learn.'

I watched.

Jolene stuck out her serviette-enhanced micro-chest and did a sexy saunter over to the corner.

Even though she's my twin, it took quite a lot of willpower to prevent myself from running after her and dragging her back by her hair.

But, still, I kept on watching. I didn't want to, but I just couldn't turn my face away. It was like car-crash TV.

I watched her jiggle her jug at River Phoenix Boy and say, 'Wanna free top-up?'

I watched him look at her and smile.

And then, suddenly, I couldn't stand any more of it. I really couldn't. It was just too horrible. Sort of like winning the lottery but then being too terrified to stand up and claim the prize.

So I looked down at the counter and began to pick a bit of egg off it. I was feeling pretty bleak if you must know. On the radio, the random DJ had stopped rambling randomly on and a song was now playing. It was some slow number about being in love with somebody who doesn't love you back. I could hear my sister laughing and making light flirty chit-chat. I squeezed my eyes shut for a second and then moved closer to one of the speakers until my ear was practically touching it. Any closer and I'd have damaged my eardrum. But it was still better than listening to Jolene and River getting it on.

I couldn't stop myself from glancing over again. Jolene was standing way too close to River Phoenix and pouring him yet another smoothie. I felt my heart sink some more and turned my attention back to the radio.

The tear-jerker was coming to a close. The singer – it must have been Adele – was wailing on and on about how she'd just have to settle for second best and find someone similar to the bloke she was in love with but couldn't have. I think it was probably the most tragically sad thing I'd ever heard in my whole life.

I heard Jolene and Drop Dead Beautiful laugh about something together. My heart was going down faster than the *Titanic*.

I stared at the damp dishcloth in my hand. And then I chucked it down on the counter and switched the radio off.

'*Love*,' I said, and curled my lip in disgust. 'You can keep it!'

At least, I *hope* I said it to myself. To be honest, it's hard to know. I was so fed up I'd reached that mad stage where I might have been mumbling out loud.

And then I heard the cafe door open and a few seconds later I heard a different voice say, 'Hi, Jody. You nearly finished in here, yeah?'

I looked up and my heart hit rock bottom.

It was Chatty Chong.

Which would have been fine if I'd wanted to talk about maths. But I didn't.

Chatty was carrying his school bag even though it was a Sunday afternoon. Plonking it down on the counter, he said, 'You wanna come and start work on our trigonometry project later, yeah?'

'Not really,' I said.

'Oh.' Chatty Chong's face fell. Then he said, 'It was my birthday yesterday. My dad gave me a brand-new graphics calculator, yeah? It's the most expensive one you can get in Argos.' He unzipped his bag and took the calculator out. It was so new that it was still inside its cardboard box. Chatty began to unpack it. 'I thought you might wanna have a go at using it, yeah? It's got built-in USB technology and everything.'

I gave the calculator a quick once-over glance and then shook my head. 'Not really,' I said. In the corner, my sister was still batting her lashes at River Phoenix. He'd got his phone out. I guessed he was taking down my sister's number.

'Oh,' said Chatty Chong, and started carefully packing his calculator up again. 'You can do scatterplots and pie-charts and everything on this calculator. It's the business, yeah?'

'Great,' I said. River Phoenix had taken a pair of massive silver headphones out of the pocket of his parka and was putting them on. This was an unexpected development. I leaned my elbows on the counter and continued to watch. Jolene stood up sharply and began walking back to the counter. She had a face like a melted welly.

Chatty Chong said, 'Ain't this a good time?'

'Not really,' I said. And then I said to Jolene, 'Everything OK?'

'I don't get it,' she hissed back in a low voice. 'I was in the middle of telling him about the Under-18 Shakedown at the Spotted Dog next week and he just put his headphones on and started playing with his phone. I hadn't even finished speaking! How utterly ignorant is that?'

She only said this to me. To Chatty Chong, she didn't say anything at all. I don't think she *means* to be utterly ignorant to Chatty – it's just that most of the time she forgets he's there. Even when he's standing right next to her.

'Maybe you were boring,' I said.

Jolene looked shocked. 'That's a bit rich! *I'm* not the one who's chatting to my boyfriend about maths, am I?' She plonked her empty smoothie jug down next to Chatty Chong's bag and added, 'I'm going upstairs. I need a break.' And then she walked over to the STAFF ONLY door, which leads up to our maisonette, and disappeared behind it with a big angry slam.

Chatty Chong scratched his head and said, 'Why'd she call me your boyfriend, yeah?' He'd gone a bit pink.

'Because she's my evil twin,' I said. I think I'd gone a bit pink too. Sometimes, I actually hate my sister.

'Oh,' said Chatty Chong. Then he said, 'And you definitely don't wanna do no maths later?'

I glanced back to the corner. River Phoenix had picked up his refilled smoothie and was drinking it through a straw. His feet had started to tap again. I wanted to know what music was coming through those huge silver headphones and making his world rock. I wanted to know that more than anything. More than the meaning of life even.

Chatty Chong frowned. 'What's up with you, Jody? Are you even listening, yeah?'

'Not really,' I said. And then I hit the side of my head with the palm of my hand and quickly added, 'I mean yeah. *Of course* I'm listening.'

Chatty put his calculator back into his bag and zipped it

up. 'Forget it, yeah? This clearly ain't a good time. Catch you laters.'

Without another word, he stomped over to the door and disappeared into the street. For a moment, I just stood still and felt bad. Chatty Chong doesn't talk to many people. I should really make a bigger effort to talk back to him.

But I didn't have a chance to feel bad for very long because the cafe door suddenly flew open again. It was my dad. He was carrying a big box of frozen turkey twizzlers and several billion cartons of juice. Even though it's February, I noticed he was sweating a lot. My dad's inner thermostat is jammed on a very high setting.

He looked over at me and said, 'All right, Sulky Sue?' And then he glanced around and said, 'Where's the other one?'

'She's upstairs having a break,' I said.

My dad put his frozen boxes down on an empty table, pulled a mobile phone out of his left pocket, pressed speed dial and said, 'Oi, Loopy Lou! Get your backside down here, pronto. I leave you on your own for half an hour and you go skipping off upstairs! Do you think I pay you to sit up there and brush your hair?'

If you didn't know my dad, you could make the mistake of thinking he's a bit of a thug. He's got a big bald head and he's nearly always wearing a Tottenham Hotspur football shirt and grumbling at us in a loud voice. But anyone who does know him would tell you that he's actually softer than a soggy Hobnob. My dad would rather walk down the street in his pyjamas than have a proper actual go at either Jolene or me. I know this for a fact because once, when my mum wanted him to shout at us for accidently racking up a bill of £82 on her iTunes account, this is exactly what he did. He walked up and down Willesden High Road for fifteen minutes in his Tottenham Hotspur pyjamas and training coat and then, when everyone had quietened down a bit, he came back and calmly worked out a way that Jolene and I could pay my mum back by doing extra cafe shifts.

Incidentally, when he's not wearing a Tottenham Hotspur football top, he's either wearing a checked shirt with a bootlace tie and a cowboy hat or an awful T-shirt that says . . .

Body by Baywatch
Face by Crimewatch

My dad is a legend. Everyone knows him and everyone likes him. And I absolutely love him. Even though he has this really random habit of calling me Sulky Sue.

'Hey, Sulky Sue,' he said to me. 'Give me a hand shifting these twizzlers.' And then he paused, nodded his head at River Phoenix and called out, 'New customer?'

River Phoenix put down his phone, pulled his silver headphones off and said, 'You what?'

'Come in here for an all-day Champion Chunky Breakfast, did you, son?'

River Phoenix said, 'Nah,' and began to put his headphones back.

My dad said, 'Whoaa there. What's this?' And he pointed to the QPR logo drawn on the sleeve of RP's parka. I held my breath. My dad can get a bit over-emotional when it comes to football.

RP looked down at his sleeve and then he grinned. 'It's the sign of a quality football club,' he said. 'Not like that cheap Spurs tat you're wearing.'

My dad's eyes widened in mock outrage. 'How can you say that! This is official clubwear! And Spurs are in the final of the League Cup this year. They'll soon have the hallowed turf of Wembley Stadium underneath their boots. I don't see QPR playing any cup finals at Wembley.'

River Phoenix shrugged. 'I'm not bothered.'

My dad shook his head and then he turned to me, winked and said, 'Jody, let's give this poor lad some orange juice. The vitamin C might do him good. He clearly ain't well because he's not thinking straight.' He picked up one of his cartons of juice and reading straight from the packaging said, 'Here you go. Orange juice. Naturally and artificially flavoured. Made from powdered concentrate.'

RP laughed again and stood up. 'Nah, you're all right. I need to get going. But thanks for the offer.' And then he looked across at me and smiled. It was the most fantastic smile I've ever seen. My body temperature rocketed and my hands went clammy. It was like being struck by lightning all over again.

I smiled back and, even though I was in the process of picking up a freezing-cold box of turkey twizzlers, I crossed my fingers on both hands and hoped for something amazing to happen. I don't know what exactly. Just some kind of random little miracle that would stop him from walking out of my life. *Anything!*

Unfortunately, it's difficult to hold a box of frozen turkey twizzlers when you've got your fingers crossed. My dad said, 'Oi, Sulky Sue – careful with those twizzlers! I don't want them going all over the floor.'

'OK,' I snapped. 'Keep your hair on!'

My dad said, 'Will do, kiddo, will do.' And then he touched his bald head and said, 'OH MY LIFE! WHERE'S IT ALL GONE?'

I laughed. It really is difficult to be annoyed with my dad for more than a couple of seconds.

My dad fished a Spurs beanie hat out of his right pocket, plonked it on his head and said, 'As soon as those twizzlers are in the freezer, you can call it a day. That lazy twin of yours can take over from here.' And with a shout of, 'Oi, Loopy Lou,' he went up the stairs to find her.

I continued to laugh and then turned back to see if the Beautiful River Phoenix Boy was laughing too. I wanted to see that fantastic smile again.

But he wasn't laughing. In fact, he wasn't even there. He'd gone.

I froze with my frozen twizzlers still in my arms. My head was filled with one horrible thought. What if I never *ever* saw him again? For a moment, I actually thought I might cry.

And then I saw it. And I realized that an amazing little miracle had happened after all.

The Beautiful Mystery Boy had left his phone on the table.

THINKING
AND
DREAMING

Titch
Calling

I looked at it. And then I picked it up. It was still slightly sweaty from being in his hands. For a second I just stood there, holding on to the sweaty phone, and then I rushed over to the front door, opened it and stepped out on to the pavement.

The world instantly changed.

Cars and buses were spluttering along the high road in both directions and people were milling around everywhere. They were walking and chatting and strutting and shouting and sometimes – in the way that drives my dad completely mental – they were hanging about by shop windows and just leaning.

I looked up the street.

Aside from all the normal types who are too yawningly

normal to describe, I could see three boys doing bunny-hops on their bikes and I could see an old lady with a shopping trolley who was weaving it around just like she thought she was Jenson Button.

I looked down the street.

Aside from a load more normals, I could see someone fast asleep on a public bench, and I could see a kid in a hoodie doing some mean keepie-uppies with an empty cola can, but I couldn't see the boy who looked like River Phoenix anywhere. It was as if he'd just walked out of the cafe and vanished.

A voice behind me said, 'Everything all right, sunshine?'

I jumped. Just as if I'd been caught doing something dodgy. I don't know why though because I hadn't been doing anything remotely dodgy at all. I'd just been looking.

It was my dad. He was back from upstairs and he had Jolene with him.

'Lost something?'

'Just getting some fresh air,' I said. The Chunky Bus choked to a halt about thirty centimetres away from my face and made me cough. I stepped back inside and quickly closed our door.

My dad winked at me. 'Look who I found upstairs – Lady Googoo singing into a pair of pink hair straighteners.' He jerked his thumb at Jolene. She was looking even more fed up than before. Quickly, I slipped the mystery boy's phone into my apron pocket.

Jolene narrowed her eyes and glared at my dad.

'Everything about that sentence is wrong! FYI, they were curling tongs – not straighteners. And it wasn't Lady Gaga I was listening to – it was Beyoncé! They're hardly similar, Dad. Actually, they're not even close to similar. Beyoncé's sound is a soulful fusion of R&B, pop, funk and hip hop whereas Lady Gaga blatantly marries electro-pop with glam-rock and heavy metal. Everybody knows that!'

My dad winked at her. (He's quite big on winking. He's not a creepy winker though.) 'That's fascinating, sweetheart,' he said. 'I'll try to remember for next time. Now, be a good girl and give the kitchen floor a quick once-over with a mop. And, Jody, get a wriggle on and get yourself out of here – you're done, sunshine.'

I didn't need telling twice. 'Thanks, Dad,' I said, and hurried over to the STAFF ONLY door.

My dad said, 'Whoaa there! Ain't you gonna take that apron off?'

I paused, one hand on the door handle and the other hovering nervously over the pocket of my hideous bright orange apron. After a second of panic, I said, 'Do I have to? I like wearing it.' And then I went very red.

My dad looked gobsmacked. But then he relaxed and said, 'Lady Googoo wearing a lot of orange this season, is she?'

'Yeah,' I said quickly.

'Like crap she is!' said Jolene. 'This season, she's mostly wearing spandex leopard print in black and silver!'

Luckily my dad ignored her. 'Well, just you make sure

you stick it in the wash before your next shift. I've got a five-star hygiene rating and I intend to keep it that way. Now jog off before I change my mind and find you something else to do.'

I did as I was told and rushed up the stairs. When I reached the locked front door of our flat, I let myself in and then ran up the next flight of stairs until I was at the very top of the building. I went straight to my bedroom, closed the door behind me and flopped down on my bed.

I lay there, breathing hard, and looked at my walls. There's a lot to look at because every square centimetre is plastered with posters – except for one rectangle above my headboard which is occupied by my prime numbers chart. And even though I've got the coolest collection of River Phoenix and Jim Morrison posters in the whole of Willesden Green, Jolene still reckons that my one single maths chart cancels out everything else and makes my entire bedroom look like a nerd hole. But that's just *her* opinion. I like it because I think prime numbers are actually fairly fascinating. And, quite frankly, I don't take much notice of what she thinks because she's got a picture of Justin Bieber on her wall.

I studied River's face. To begin with, it was a very calming thing to do. His green eyes were deep and intense and his cheekbones were so sharp that they looked as if they'd been carefully calculated with a protractor. In fact, I'd say that River Phoenix was so good-looking that it's impossible not to fall in love with him a little bit. Even though he's just a poster on my wall. Even though he's dead. Even though . . .

I'd stopped feeling calm and started feeling a bit agitated so I shifted my focus to my prime numbers chart and studied that for a while and then, when I'd lost interest in that, I stood up and walked over to the window. I pressed my face to the glass. It smelt fusty and damp. Further down the street, the white arch of Wembley was shooting through the sky, and thin shafts of February afternoon sunshine were bouncing against it. It actually looked like it was glowing. That's why I really love that arch. It's different every single time you see it. And it always makes me feel happy. Even if I'm in a really bog-awful mood. I don't know why it has this effect on me. But, as long as I can see that great big steel rainbow, I know that nothing is anywhere near as bog-awful as it seems.

I took the phone out of my apron pocket and had a proper look at it. It was a nice one. With a touch-screen and a shiny silver shell. And, even though the screen had a crack in it and the whole thing was held together with a piece of sticky tape, it was still way cooler than the matching pay-as-you-go supermarket Shame Boxes that me and Jolene have to put up with.

The boy's phone felt weird in my hand. Or maybe it was just my hand that was feeling weird. It had gone all clammy.

I put the phone down on the window sill. And then I just stood there, leaning against the window and drumming my fingers on the wooden sill. And then I picked the phone up again.

It still felt weird. But it felt sort of nice too. Sort of dangerously and temptingly nice. I quickly put it down.

I pressed my face back to the window. The Wembley arch was still there. Everything was OK. I took a deep breath, snatched the phone up again and switched it on. The screen glowed and buzzed into life. After a couple of seconds, the blank surface was replaced with a set of tiny icons. Carefully, to avoid doing any more damage to the cracked screen, I touched the icon for the main menu. Then I touched the one for the phone log. A load of names and numbers appeared on the screen. I quickly switched it off.

This felt bad. Really bad. Like looking through somebody's sock drawer or something.

But, then again, you have to ask yourself this question:

Is it wrong to look through somebody's sock drawer if you're trying to find a way to return their phone to them?

I switched the phone back on. Hardly daring to breathe, I quickly scanned the list of contacts. There were names like Waggy and Rory and Spoony and Kyle. The last number dialled had been to someone called Titch. He didn't sound too scary. Before I could change my mind, I pressed redial and waited.

Somewhere, a phone began to ring.

I waited. Only for a second or two. And then somebody who sounded exactly like a gangster said, 'Hey, Liam, what's up?'

Quick as a flash, I pressed end call. And then I sat back down on my bed and smiled.

Liam.

Liam. Liam. Liam. Liam.

The phone began to flash and vibrate in my hand. I dropped it on my duvet as if I'd been burned. Titch's name was flashing on the screen. He obviously wanted to chat.

'No way,' I muttered. I know it's shallow to make judgements based on first impressions, but sometimes you just can't help it. And Titch had sounded dead shifty to me.

I waited. After another second, the phone went silent and the screen went dull. Titch blatantly wasn't the sort of person who liked to hang about. I picked the phone up again and navigated my way back to the list of contacts. There was one called Mum. This seemed like safer territory. I selected the option for dial number and waited.

After a few rings, a woman answered and said, 'Hi, Liam.'

'No,' I said quickly. 'I'm not Liam. But I need to get hold of him. I've got his phone, you see. He left it at my dad's cafe.'

I heard Liam's mum make an exasperated noise that sounded something like 'Puh!'. And then she said, 'Sounds about right. He's so forgetful he'd leave his brain behind if it wasn't trapped inside his head.'

She was Irish. I could tell it from her accent. So Liam was Irish then. Or *half* Irish. An image of the actor Colin Farrell flashed through my head. Because he's Irish as well.

And then I got thinking about another Irish actor – Jonathan Rhys Meyers . . .

. . . And then my head started to boggle a bit.

There was another blast of exasperated breath down the phone. And then she said, 'Well, thanks. He should be home any moment. Soon as he gets in, I'll pass the message on and tell him to drop by. What did you say the cafe was called?'

'Chunky's Diner,' I said. 'But . . . but . . .' I stopped for a moment. My hands were so sweaty they felt like they were melting.

'Yes?' said Liam's mum.

'Er . . . well . . .' I was starting to feel shiftier than Titch. 'Could you get him to ring me on his phone before he drops by? So I know when he's coming. Because a lot of the time we're shut.'

I'm a rubbish liar – I know I am. And I also know that my dad would be totally outraged if he ever learned of this particular lie. Because our cafe is hardly *ever* shut. In fact, the only days we don't open are Christmas Day and Boxing Day. But luckily for me my dad was two floors below and well out of earshot.

Liam's mum sounded a bit doubtful. 'OK, love, I'll get him to call you. But listen to me, kiddo, if I find out that you've been using that phone to chat to all your friends, it won't be my Liam you have to answer to – it'll be me. Have you got that?'

'Yes,' I said. Because I had. And then I said, 'I won't.' And I meant it.

We both said bye and then I just sat in silence staring at the phone. I don't know how long I sat like that, but it was long enough to give me boringitis and backache. I stood up, stretched, leaned over to my mega-bass super-woofer and switched it on. Flicking through my MP3 files, I selected The Doors and then 'Light My Fire' and turned the volume right up. Instantly, the cheerfully weird sound of Ray Manzarek's electronic organ filled my room. Ray was the keyboard player in The Doors. He wasn't anywhere near as good-looking or as cool as Jim Morrison, but he had fingers that could skip across a keyboard like a spring lamb on a grassy hillside. Probably he still does because as far as I'm aware he's actually managed to stay alive.

Listening to The Doors made me feel better. I rolled over on to my side, curled up into a ball and closed my eyes. Jim Morrison started to sing. I curled up tighter and listened.

His voice was soft and deep and hypnotic and beautiful.

And, even though I really didn't want to go there, I suddenly found myself transported back downstairs. And I was standing at the counter and looking over at the boy in the corner. And I was moving a few steps sideways so that I could see him better, and when I did it felt just as if I'd been struck by lightning. All. Over. Again.

My eyes snapped open.

What if Liam phoned me while this music was on and I didn't hear him?

I got up and turned the volume down on my mega-bass super-woofer. And then, just to be on the safe side, I turned it off altogether.

But a quick glance at the phone told me that Liam hadn't

rung. It was still lying silent and lifeless on top of my bed. No messages were scrolling across the screen to tell me I'd missed any calls. Not even Titch had rung. I picked the phone up and carried it over to my desk. Then I sat down and drummed my fingers against my desktop for a bit. When I got fed up with doing that, I stopped, took my maths project out of the desk drawer and opened it. I stared at it for a while. And then I sighed, closed it and shoved it back in the drawer.

I put my head down on my desk.

And finally, at long last, the phone burst into noisy life and a blast of a ringtone filled my room. I recognized it at once. It was an old R&B song called 'Return of the Mack'. This was a big hit around about the time that Jolene and I were born and the only reason I know it is because my dad sings it sometimes when he's been out to the pub and comes swaggering back home. Except that he sings 'Return of the *Mike*', because even though everybody calls him Chunky my dad's real name is actually Michael.

Personally, I wouldn't ever have guessed that 'Return of the Mack' was Liam's cup of tea. To be honest though, nothing much was surprising me any more.

I snatched the phone up. The word Mum was flashing on the screen. My heart sank. I wasn't in the mood for another conversation with her. Reluctantly, I pressed accept and said, 'Hello?'

A boy's voice said, 'So you've got my phone then?'

My heart shot upward into my mouth. And then it did a

backflip, a side-spin and a quick moonwalk before swallow-diving downward and settling in my throat like a great big awkward lump.

I gulped. And then I said, 'Yeah.' Except that it didn't actually sound like 'yeah'. It actually sounded like a yelp. As if someone wearing bovver-boots had stomped on my overly-long little toe while I was wearing flip-flops. I slapped my palm across my forehead and let out a silent inner scream.

Liam said, 'So will you be open after school tomorrow then?'

'Yeah,' I said. I managed to say it properly this time.

Liam said, 'You don't say much, do you?'

'No,' I said. Because he was dead right. For some reason, I was suddenly less chatty than Chatty Chong on a sponsored silence. Which was weird. Because actually there was loads of stuff I wanted to say to him. Questions mostly. Questions like . . .

Do you like Jim Morrison? What were you listening to on those massive silver headphones? What's your last name? Where do you live?

Which school do you go to? Why have I never seen you before? Are you aware that you look just like River Phoenix? Where did you learn to look so flipping hipping cool? When can I see you again?

But I couldn't ask him any of those questions because my jaw had gone stiff.

Liam said, 'So how about I drop by straight after school? Be about fourish?'

'Yes,' I said. And then I remembered that Monday after school is always Maths Club. Normally I never miss it. In fact, me and Chatty Chong *are* Mrs Hamood's Maths Club.

'No problem,' I said. 'And don't worry about your phone, – I'll look after it.'

'Cheers,' said Liam. And then he paused and said, 'What did you say your name was again?'

'Jo.'

'See you tomorrow then, Jo,' said Liam. And he rang off.

I held his phone in my hand, leaned back in my chair and thought about Liam's voice. It was soft but slightly gruff. Confident but not cocky. Breezy. Boyish. Beautiful. Liam had a beautiful voice. Just like Jim Morrison.

I sat there for about an hour just thinking about that.

Finally, somewhere below, I heard footsteps and I knew that the time for thinking and dreaming was over. After all, thinking and dreaming can only get you so far in life. Actions are what really matter. And if you're not in a position to take action or don't dare to it's best not to torture yourself.

I firmly pushed all thoughts of Liam and his beautiful face and his geometric cheekbones and his lovely voice out of my head. And then I stood up, poked my head into the hallway and shouted, 'Jolene? Is that you?'

My sister's voice floated up the stairs. 'Well, it's hardly Dad, is it? Can you feel the floor shaking?' She clearly hadn't cheered up.

'Dad's not *that* fat,' I said defensively. 'And, anyway, you might have been Mum. She's due back from The Talon Salon about now. Anyway, come up here a moment, will you? I need to show you something.'

I waited. Jolene's footsteps thumped upward. I took a deep breath and held it until she reached the top.

A moment later, Jolene plonked herself down on my bed and said, 'So what's up?'

I didn't answer her straight away. I think I waited for about a second. And in that second, I could hear a voice in my head saying, 'You really don't have to do this! She doesn't own him or anything. You do NOT have to do this!'

But I knew I *did* have to do it. Because it was the only thing to do.

And she's my twin. And she spotted Liam first. And, to be perfectly honest, the whole situation was so complicated that it was making my brain melt.

It was a very long second.

And then I put the phone in Jolene's hand and said, 'His name is Liam. And he's coming to the cafe at four o'clock tomorrow to get this back. And you're going to be there to stun him with your full charm offensive when he does.'

ONE CAREFUL DRIVER

One thing I've learned in maths is that it's mostly about patterns. Right back as far as Reception class, I've been filling my head up with them. To begin with, it was easy patterns like 2, 4, 6, 8 . . . but then by the time I was in Year 4 I could do trickier ones like 8, 16, 24, 32 . . . And then when I got to high school Mrs Hamood introduced me to a whole load more of them. She taught me about square numbers and cube numbers and the Fibonacci sequence and Kaprekar's sequence and Pascal's triangle and Penrose's tiling pattern, and I could go on and on talking like this forever because you can never really run out of patterns and sequences in maths. And, anyway, you can always have a go at making up a few of your own. Or, if you're a daydreamer like me, you can do what I do and just draw pictures in your maths book until the lesson ends.

Interestingly, there is no logical pattern to prime numbers. As far as I can tell, primes appear along the number line completely at random. This is probably why I find them fascinating.

But patterns don't just happen in maths. They happen in life too. All the time. In fact, my life pretty much follows one great big massive pattern. During the week, I get up at seven, have a shower and eat my breakfast, and then I brush my teeth and walk to school with Jolene. When I'm there, I follow a timetable, which is the same every single week, and then I come home and work for a couple of hours in the cafe and then I do whatever I like for the rest of the evening. Sometimes I might go to Maths Club – if it's a Monday – or I might work on my project with Chatty Chong or I might hang out with Jolene at Brent Cross Shopping Centre or walk down to Kilburn Market and talk to the nice woman who sells me posters of River Phoenix and The Doors. And, even though my life might not seem fantastically spectacular, I almost never get bored. Because I like these recurring patterns. It means that everything in my world is ticking along nicely.

But after Liam left his phone in our cafe I started to behave a lot more randomly.

Normally, I don't do much on Sunday evenings. There's not really anything very interesting to do and there's never anything much cop on telly. So usually I just stay in my room and play on my Xbox or go to Jolene's room and play on hers. And sometimes, if we want to play each other but can't be bothered to leave the comfort of our own individual rooms, we put on these hysterical wi-fi gaming helmets that my dad got cheap from Frosty Frank and we zap the crap out of each other that way.

But the other Sunday I didn't do either of those things. After setting my sister up with the boy who had blown my mind, I just lay on my bed for about three hours and looked at my posters. And, even though Jolene barged into my room four times to challenge me to a game of Call of Duty, I didn't budge. In the end, I told her I had a headache and, eventually, she took the hint and left me alone.

I didn't have a headache though. I was just discovering what the word heartache meant.

And then on Monday everything went even more random. Jolene and I were walking to school and everything was fine until Natalie Snell and Latasha Joy rocked up and started walking with us. Natalie Snell is the hardest girl in my school and Latasha Joy thinks she's it just because she's got bigger bazookas than Dolly Parton.

I don't like either of them.

And they don't like me because I'm quiet and good at maths.

They like Jolene though because she's crap at maths and good at netball. And, to be fair, everyone likes Jolene.

Natalie Snell said, 'All riiiiiight twinny twin twinnies!'

Latasha Joy pushed her bazookas out and said, 'What's up?'

And Jolene suddenly acquired this fake gangster accent and said, 'Heeeeyyyy, wassup, sisters?'

And I just sort of smiled and didn't say anything because I didn't really want them to be there.

Natalie Snell ignored me and said, 'Been meaning to catch up with you, yeah, Joles. There's this guy in my geography class that's got the hots for you big time! Tyler Smith. D'you know him?'

Latasha Joy pushed her bazookas out and said, 'He's Nat's cousin, innit.'

And Jolene laughed and said, 'Flattered, yeah. But I ain't interested. Soz.'

And I just kept walking and looked at my feet because I hate these kind of conversations.

Natalie Snell frowned. And then she said, 'What's wrong with Tyler?'

Latasha Joy said, 'Yeah, wassup with him? You got a problem with his face or something?'

And Jolene said, 'No! There's nothing wrong with his face. Relaaax! I'm just well into someone else right now.'

And I sighed but nobody heard me because nobody was paying any attention to me.

Natalie Snell's eyes went big and round and interested. 'Who is it?'

Jolene said, 'He's called Liam. He doesn't go to our school. He's fitter than a McFitty biscuit.'

I cringed. Jolene commits really chronic word abuse sometimes.

Natalie Snell said, 'Wow! So you're saying he's even buffer than my own blood relation, is it?'

Latasha Joy wiggled around behind her big bazookas and said, 'Ain't no bloke more nang than Nat's cousin, is it?'

My crazy sister Jolene just laughed really casually as if she didn't have a worry in the world and said, 'I ain't saying Tyler ain't good-looking or nothing. Cos he blatantly is. But I just ain't into him right now. Cos this Liam guy is raaaaaaw!'

And then, after a nasty moment where I truly thought Jolene might get beaten to a pulp for disrespecting Natalie Snell's blood relation, all three of them relaxed and started laughing and cackling and crowing on and on about how completely fit and buff and nang and raw Liam was.

And although I didn't exactly disagree with them I couldn't easily join in. And, anyway, I didn't want to. It seemed a bit disrespectful and tasteless somehow.

In fact, I just wanted to get as far away from all three of them as I could.

So, for the first time in my entire life, I decided to break my Monday pattern and do something I'd never ever done before in my whole fifteen years and eleven months of existence – although that's actually only three genuine birthdays, remember.

I decided to bunk off school.

I didn't spend ages thinking it through. Actually, I didn't even think it through at all. I just pulled Jolene back by her arm and said, 'You know what – I don't fancy going in today. But don't say anything to Mum and Dad though, will you?'

Jolene looked shocked. Even Natalie and Latasha looked a bit surprised.

'Why?'

'I ain't done my extended maths homework,' I lied. 'I don't wanna get any grief from Mrs Hamood.'

Jolene frowned. 'I didn't even know we *had* any maths homework. You haven't done any for *me*. Does that mean I'm going to get a load of grief as well?'

'No,' I said. 'This is *extended* maths homework. Only me and Chatty Chong had to do it.' I was speaking at about a million miles per hour. I tend to do that when I'm lying.

Jolene laughed. 'As if you'd get any grief from *her*! She totally loves you!'

I shrugged. 'I just don't feel like going in,' I said. And then, without another word, I did a 180° turn and walked back towards Willesden High Road.

Above the noise of the buses and cars, I heard Jolene shout after me a couple of times – but I just kept right on walking. I needed to be on my own. This can happen occasionally when you're a twin.

There was no way I was going home though. Because I knew my mum and dad would be in the cafe and that my mum would insist on dragging me over to the doctor's surgery the very second I tried spinning her any sort of rubbish story about being sick or something.

(FYI, our family doctor is called Dr Rash and practically

every time I've ever had to see him I've left the surgery with a little plastic bottle to wee in and a prescription for those pills that have to be inserted via the back door. To be honest, I'd rather just go to school.)

So I completely avoided Willesden High Road and carried on walking until I got to Gladstone Park and then I sat down on a bench and stared at the ducks.

Gladstone Park is nice. It's a massive green space that touches the edges of Willesden Green and Neasden and Cricklewood – and that's a really good thing because we don't have many massive green spaces. To be honest, we don't have many little ones either. The other good things about Gladstone Park are the hill in the middle of it, which gives you a really smart view of the whole of Wembley stadium – not just the arch – and the big duck pond on the top of the hill. The only bad thing about the park is that my school sometimes forces us to do cross-country running all the flipping way round it.

Luckily, Year 11 doesn't have PE or games on a Monday so I was able to sit and stare at the ducks in total peace.

I couldn't even hear any buses for once.

I've no idea how long I sat there. I gave the ducks my sandwiches. They were cheese and tomato and the ducks seemed to like them quite a lot. Especially the ones with the emerald-green heads. Then, after a while, I stood up and leaned against the pond railings so that I could watch the ducks push and shove each other out of the way to get to my shredded sarnies. And it was while I was doing this that

I became aware of a really very weird sensation rolling around inside my head and in my belly. And it was this:

Yes. I was jealous of the ducks!

Because it suddenly occurred to me that being born a duck is a whole lot less complicated and a whole lot less stressful than being born a human being. Even for twin ducks. After all, the biggest thing they ever have to worry about is grabbing a piece of bread before any other duck does.

I bet *they* don't ever get into a flap about love and loyalty and doing the right twinny thing. And I bet they don't get themselves into a state because they can't stop thinking about the wrong duck.

After thinking that, I didn't want to look at them any more, because being jealous of a bunch of flipping ducks doesn't make you feel that great about yourself, if I'm honest.

So I left the park and walked back towards Willesden High Road and this meant that I had to use the footbridge that crosses the train tracks by Dollis Hill tube station. And rather than walk straight across the footbridge like I normally do I did another random thing. I walked as far as the middle of the bridge and then I stopped. Don't ask me why I stopped, because I don't actually know. It was just another unpredictable act that followed no particular kind of pattern.

And then I stood there for about twenty-five minutes, with my chin resting on the top of the railing, and watched the tube trains coming and going beneath me. You can do this in my part of London. Because this far out of the centre the tube trains don't actually travel through tubes.

And, even though I've always thought that trainspotters are a seriously weird bunch of people, I'm now wondering if, *actually*, they're on to something very interesting. Because my twenty-five minutes on the footbridge were totally and utterly fascinating. And for a while I think I even forgot to feel messed up and confused about Liam.

Very quickly, I saw a strict pattern emerging. Firstly, a train would pull slowly out of Dollis Hill station and rumble away towards the West End. As it curved round a bend in the track, I could see that a few passengers were reading paperbacks and newspapers, but mostly they were just staring into space.

And then, about two or three minutes after I'd lost sight of that train, another one, on a parallel track and heading *back* from the West End, would crawl into Dollis Hill station and stop with a big hiss right beneath my feet. There were never many people on these trains either.

But the trains that interested me the most were the ones which passed by on a *third* piece of track set slightly over to one side. These were the high-speed trains on the Metropolitan line, and they whizzed through Dollis Hill station without even stopping. Every six minutes, the track began to rattle and hum, and seconds later a blur of red, white and blue metal raced by underneath me. I've got no way of knowing whether the passengers inside were reading newspapers or staring into space or whether there was actually a single person on board or not, because the trains were moving much too fast for me to take a look inside.

But I do know that I definitely wouldn't want to get in the way.

Because those things could do some seriously nasty damage.

And that got me thinking about just how vitally important maths is. Because, without the careful sequencing of trains going in and out of Dollis Hill tube station, it's fair to say that there would be total and utter carnage. But it also got me thinking about how vitally important and skilled and alert those train drivers have to be. Because they've got a serious amount of responsibility sitting on their shoulders. They're the only ones who have the power to prevent a really catastrophic collision.

And all at once I realized that I absolutely, necessarily

and categorically needed to stop giving this mysterious Liam ANY of my headspace at all.

In actual fact, I couldn't even understand why I *still* was. It was like he had morphed into some kind of weird boomerang. I kept throwing him out of my brain and he kept flying straight back in again.

But I had to find a way of shutting him out of my head completely. Because even *thinking* about him was dangerous. Thinking about him made me want to be with him.

Just like Jolene wanted to be with him.

And if I didn't back right off, me and her were inevitably going to wind up in a really ugly and hideous collision.

In fact, if I didn't back right off, I was in serious danger of getting myself into something I couldn't really cope with.

And, just like the tube-train drivers, I was the only person who had the power to prevent this from happening.

It was a big responsibility.

RETURN OF THE MACK

So I should have stayed right away from the cafe that afternoon. I should have gone to Maths Club like I normally do on Mondays and played lame games on the computer, which have names like Sonic the Hexagon or Super Mario Cartesian Co-ordinates, and helped little kids in Year 7 with their maths homework. But I couldn't do any of that because I'd skipped off school. And as I was cold and a bit bored and as it had started to rain and as I had absolutely nothing else to do, I stayed out until 3 p.m. and then I went back home.

I suppose it's fair to say that I'm not much good at skipping school.

My mum was behind the counter when I got back. She always is on Mondays. It's my dad's only day off, and every

Monday afternoon he gets on the train with Frosty Frank and they travel all the way to Romford in Essex just to watch greyhounds race each other round a track. My dad reckons it's like going to a gym but better. Because the greyhounds run much faster than he ever could and gambling is a much easier way to lose a few pounds.

Like I said before, my dad is a very funny man.

My mum gave me a massive smile and said, 'You're home early! Where's your sister?'

And I said, 'Maths Club was cancelled.' And then I said, 'I don't flipping well know where she is. We might be twins, but that doesn't mean we're joined at the hip.'

My mum said, 'Oooh, what's up with you?' And then she put her hands behind her back to untie her apron and said, 'Be an angel, will you? Now you're here, you couldn't just keep an eye on the cafe for me while I nip across the road and top my tan up?'

'Oh, Mummm,' I said.

'I'll pay you double bubble,' said my mum. 'It's hardly busy in here. And, anyway, Jolene will be home any second so you won't be on your own.'

And, even though I'd decided that I definitely was not going to be about when Liam rocked up to collect his phone, I agreed. Because double bubble is a very difficult offer to turn down.

And the truth is that, however much I told myself I didn't want to see Liam, I knew that, deep deep down, I very seriously did.

So I pulled an orange apron over my head, plonked myself down on a stool behind the counter and fixed my eyes on the clock on the wall.

And I waited.

At 3.41, Jolene rushed in, rushed over to me, said, 'I can't believe you bunked off school today! We'll talk about it later,' and then rushed upstairs to make herself look beautiful for Liam.

At 3.57, she came down again. She'd swapped her school uniform for her Chunky's Diner uniform and some make-up. It wasn't ideal, but she still looked quite nice.

At 4.00, Liam didn't arrive.

'Oh crap,' said Jolene. 'Do you think he's gonna come?'

I rolled my eyes. 'He said *about* four o'clock. It's only four o'clock now. Give him a chance.'

At 4.32, Liam still hadn't arrived so Jolene rushed upstairs to freshen up.

At 4.43, she came down again. Personally, I thought she looked slightly less nice than she did before.

There was still no sign of Liam.

At 5.06, Jolene rushed upstairs to reapply her make-up. If she'd asked for my advice, I'd have told her not to bother. She'd already blatantly overdone the black eye-gunk as it was. Her eyelids were practically collapsing under the stuff. But as usual she hadn't asked for my advice. She never does about make-up. Only about maths homework.

At 5.14, the front door of the cafe opened.

It was him!

My stomach did a somersault.

Apart from Whispering Bob Harris and a couple of old ladies who were taking advantage of the Chunky's Diner BOGOF on pensioner meals, it was just the two of us. My mum was still across the road at A Tan for All Seasons and Jolene was still putting on more make-up. Unfortunately, I was in the middle of scoffing a sneaky fried-egg sandwich. Liam looked over and waved at me at the exact same moment that I stuck my tongue out to stop runny egg yolk dribbling down my chin.

I'm beginning to understand why there has never been a queue of people desperate to go out with me.

Liam was wearing the moss-green parka again. I don't believe there's anyone in the world who looks as good in a moss-green parka as he does. Underneath it, I could see a fraction of his school uniform. But not enough to see which school he actually went to. He was wet from the rain and his trousers were soggy where they'd dragged on the ground. I could tell that they'd been deliberately unstitched at the hems to make them as long as possible. Most people would look skanky in unstitched trousers like that. But not him.

He crossed over to the counter and said, 'Hi. You've got my phone I think.' And then he said, 'You missed a bit,' and tapped his own chin to show me where I'd still got egg stuck to mine.

My hand flew up to my face.

Liam grinned and said, 'Got you! I'm just kidding. Your face is fine.'

He was looking right at me. He thought my face was fine! I looked back at him and smiled. And in that second, I got a clear view of his eyes. Even though he has River Phoenix's face, his eyes are completely different. River's eyes were green. (I've got no idea what colour Jim Morrison's eyes were, because all the posters I have of him are black and white.)

But Liam has eyes the colour of conkers.

And his eyelashes are amazing too. You wouldn't normally think that eyelashes could be particularly amazing, but his are. They're long and curly and they look nice. Jolene's eyelashes never look as nice as his even though she uses a lorry-load of mascara.

But then I bit my lip and looked at the floor. Without risking another look at him, I said, 'Actually it's not me you want, it's my sister. She's just popped upstairs. I'll give her a shout.'

Liam looked surprised. 'Didn't sound like your sister I spoke to on the blower. Sounded exactly like you.'

I shook my head. 'No, it was definitely her. We're twins.'

'Even so . . .' said Liam. But I didn't let him finish. I hurried over to the STAFF ONLY door, opened it and yelled up, 'Jolene, the guy for the phone is here.'

When my sister feels like it, she's got bionic hearing. From somewhere way up higher I heard our front door open and Jolene shout back, 'Ohmigodohmigodohmigod,' and then I heard the thump of her feet on the stairs.

Without another glance in Liam's direction, I said,

'This is her now,' and scarpered.

Whispering Bob Harris was eating ham, egg and chips in one of the window seats. I noticed that *his* egg had been giving him grief as well. He'd dripped it all over the table. I grabbed a cloth and said, 'Would you like me to wipe that for you, sir?'

WBH cupped his hand behind his ear and said, 'Speak up, son. I can't hear you.'

I smiled. I always do when he says this. For some reason, it just totally tickles my pickles. He even calls my mum son. I waved my cloth at him and wiped the table. I was still doing this when, behind me, Jolene announced her arrival with a big cheery 'Hiya'.

I heard Liam say hi back.

'Hi-de-flipping-hi,' I muttered into my dishcloth. To be honest, I was starting to feel really crap. It's not easy being nice and setting your sister up with a boy who looks like River Phoenix. In fact, it wouldn't surprise me if it's one of the hardest things to do in the whole world. I reckon it's even more difficult than Fermat's Last Theorem – and, according to the *Guinness Book of World Records*, Fermat's Last Theorem is the most difficult maths problem in the entire history of maths. Except that Mr Fermat did eventually come up with an answer so it wasn't that blinking tricky.

'Speak up, son. I can't hear you,' bellowed Whispering Bob Harris.

'I didn't say anything,' I bellowed back.

Whispering Bob Harris put his hand up to his mouth as if he wanted to tell me a secret, leaned forward and thundered, 'What the heck is that one over there wearing? She's forgotten her blinking trousers!' And then he nodded his head in Jolene's direction.

I turned round.

Instantly, my jaw dropped and my heart sank. *I'd* just done something really generous and unselfish. For her. For her to have another chance with Luscious Liam. And she'd already blown it.

And then my mouth closed and my heart lifted right up. Good, I thought. Good. Good. Good.

And then my heart sank again. Because I didn't feel good at all. I felt guilty.

Jolene hadn't only tampered with her make-up – she'd tampered with her clothes too. And for someone who's had more hot dates than an African calendar she'd got her entire look completely wrong. The usual Chunky's uniform – orange apron, orange T-shirt and black trousers – had been ditched in favour of a pink crop top and a pair of silver shorts which were so short that, on first glance, it looked as if she'd just wrapped a bit of baking foil round her bum.

Beyoncé Knowles could easily get away with this, but Jolene Barton just looked stupid.

Weirdest of all, though, were the socks she was wearing. They had blue and white stripes on and were pulled up high over her knees.

Queens Park Rangers football socks.

I shook my head and moved on to wipe another table. Jolene was blatantly trying way too hard. Anyone with eyes could see that Liam is not the type of person to get excited by a tragic Trudy Try-Hard.

Whispering Bob Harris bellowed, 'Service please!'

I chucked my cloth down and went back to see what he wanted. He had the wipe-clean menu open in front of him.

I said, 'How can I help you, sir?'

WBH said, 'Speak up, son. I can't hear you!' And then he tapped a picture of a slice of apple pie and bellowed, 'And custard. And a cuppa tea.'

This time my pickles weren't tickled. In fact, I was feeling thoroughly fed up. Before I could think about what I was saying, I bellowed back, 'No problem, son.' And then, immediately, I felt ashamed for disrespecting someone who is older than God. Then I remembered that WBH can't hear anyway and felt OK again.

But as I began to walk off he bellowed, 'What the bloody hell is up with you today?' So I'm not actually sure whether he heard me or not.

Liam was leaning against the counter and talking to Jolene. He had a silly grin on his lovely face. She had one on hers too. I know for a fact that there wasn't one on mine. I opened the fridge, took out a slice of apple pie, whacked it into a dish and then slammed the whole lot into the microwave. Being a good twin and doing a seriously unselfish thing is not something I can wholeheartedly recommend.

I heard Liam say, 'You sound totally different in real

life to how you do on the phone.'

And I heard Jolene say, 'Yeah, well, yesterday I had a snotty cold.'

I took a can of custard out of the cupboard, attacked it with a can-opener and pretended that it was Jolene's head.

Liam said, 'So can I have my phone back then?'

Jolene said, 'Yeah. It's in my dad's office. I'll go and get it. So what's your name? Liam what?'

I stopped attacking the can so that I could listen better.

'Mackie,' said Liam.

So that explained the ringtone. 'Return of the Mack'.

Jolene said, 'Which school do you go to?'

Liam grinned and pulled a face. 'What is this? Twenty questions?'

'I'm just asking,' stropped Jolene. 'I didn't realize I needed some sort of licence! Jeez!'

I smiled and set back to work on the can of custard.

Liam said, 'Hey, I like your socks. So you're a QPR fan?'

Jolene's voice brightened right up. 'Oh yeah, I love them. Best football team in the whole of London.'

I smiled again. In fact, I nearly laughed out loud. I have to hand it to Jolene. If there's something she really, really wants, she makes a proper effort to go out and get it. Having those words in her mouth must have made her want to vom.

Liam said, 'It's funny that. Because you've got the Spurs logo all over your nails.'

I closed my eyes. She makes a proper effort. But she's also a proper muppet.

But then again she's also my twin sister and listening to her massively FAIL with the bloke of her dreams was beginning to make me feel pretty awkward and uncomfortable.

I turned round and said, 'For your information, we're a two-team family. Spurs and QPR. Always have been. Always will be.'

'Your dad didn't seem like much of a QPR fan,' said Liam.

'He's not,' I said. 'But my mum is. And so are me and Jolene.'

Jolene looked at me and smiled. And it was such a grateful smile that, for a second, I wanted to cry. When all is said and done, nobody could ever come between me and her. Not even Liam Mackie.

Liam smiled at me too. 'Fair enough. So maybe I'll see you at a Rangers match one day.'

My heart stopped. Had he just said that to me? To be honest, I hate football. Normally, I'd rather shave my eyeballs than watch an entire game. But if he was asking . . .

Jolene said, 'Cool! When are they playing next? We could combine it with a burger somewhere and then maybe go on to the cinema afterwards and catch a film. I really want to see *Mothello*. It's a 3D cartoon tragedy involving a massively jealous moth. I don't know you yet, Liam, but my guess is that you'd completely love it. So what do you say?'

My sister may be a muppet. But she's an über-confident one.

Liam smiled again. And then he started to laugh. 'Cartoon moths? Nah, I don't think so. Can I have my phone back though?'

The microwave pinged. I took WBH's apple pie out and poured cold custard over it. And then I put it back in.

Jolene said, 'I'll get your phone, shall I?'

I didn't need to look at her to know that she was properly cheesed off. Her voice had turned so frosty that she sounded like she could spit ice cubes. My sister Jolene doesn't like being knocked back. Especially not *twice* in two days from the exact same guy.

Without another word, she went off to get Liam's phone from the tiny cupboard underneath the stairs that my dad calls his OPERATIONS OFFICE.

Liam folded his arms on the counter and grinned at me. 'No offence to your sister,' he said. 'She just ain't my type.'

'Oh,' I said.

Liam laughed again and said, 'Does she do the talking for both of you?'

I didn't say anything. I couldn't. My voice-box had packed up. And actually this was massively inconvenient because if it had been working I'd have used it to shout,

'What about me, Liam? Am *I* your type?'

But because I was speechless I just went all hot and prickly and stared at the microwave and felt massively humongously and incredibly awkward.

For a moment, the only things that could be heard at our end of the cafe were the whirring of the microwave and a particularly loud conversation between the two BOGOF old ladies who were sitting close to the counter. They were so old that it's possible they were even older than Whispering Bob Harris. They were talking about childbirth. One of them said, 'Do you know what, Doreen? Fourteen hours I was in labour with my Bobby. *Fourteen hours!* And he had a head like an oversized watermelon. I don't know how I managed. I'll tell you one thing for sure, though, I ain't ever going through all that again!'

The other old lady said, 'Well, Vee, you don't need to tell me about pain. When I had my Carol, it turned out that my trapdoor weren't big enough. The midwife had to–'

I rushed to the stereo and pressed play on the MP3. The sound of Johnny Cash filled the cafe. My dad's favourite. Not mine though. In my opinion, Johnny Cash's voice is shiftier than Titch's and twice as terrifying. I switched the stereo off again.

Liam said, 'Hey, can't you leave that on? Johnny Cash is a dude!'

My eyebrows shot off the top of my head, but I switched Johnny Cash back on again. To be fair, perhaps I've never really given him a proper listen.

The front door opened and, briefly, the noise of cars and

buses splashing down Willesden High Road in the rain mixed into the general Johnny Cash versus Childbirth Horror Story audio mash-up. I looked up and then immediately wished I hadn't. Chatty Chong was walking towards me.

Chatty Chong plonked his school bag down on the counter. Then, after a suspicious sideways glance at Liam Mackie, he said, 'You weren't in Maths Club, yeah?'

'No,' I said. Although, to be strictly honest, I didn't really *say* it. It was more of a mortified *mumble*.

Liam Mackie grinned and said, 'Maths Club? Rock and roll!'

My face started burning. Chatty Chong shot another suspicious sideways glance at Liam and then he said, 'Come to think of it, you weren't in maths either.'

I didn't say anything. I just frowned at Chatty Chong and telepathically told him to clear off.

He didn't clear off though. Instead, he said, 'So what time do you finish in here? Do you wanna come over to mine after and draw some isosceles triangles, yeah?'

'Not really,' I mumbled.

Liam's eyes boggled. Shaking his head in amazement, he said, 'Do you wanna draw some isosceles triangles?' And then he started laughing so hard that he had to put his head down on the counter.

I turned away and stared at WBH's apple pie and custard. According to the timer on the microwave, it still needed another minute and forty seconds. Not that I actually needed a poxy microwave to warm anything up – I could have just used the heat from my face.

Chatty Chong said, 'Ain't this a good time?'

'Not really,' I said.

Chatty Chong was silent for a second. He gave a long, hard look at Liam Mackie and then he gave a long, hard look at me. And then, after what felt like a solid hour of long, hard looking, he picked up his bag and walked out of the cafe.

'Rock and roll,' said Liam again, and he began to sing along to the Johnny Cash song playing on the stereo. It was a song about a boy called Sue. It's probably my least favourite song of all time.

During a quiet bit in the record, I heard the old lady called Vee say to the old lady called Doreen, 'Does your trapdoor still give you trouble? Mine does on odd occasions.'

But to my relief I never got to hear Doreen's reply because the front door opened again. My mum was back from the tanning salon.

'Hiya, baby,' she said, and waved at me.

'Hiya, Mum,' I said, and waved back. I don't think I've ever been so glad to see her in my whole life. I didn't even mind too much that she'd called me baby.

The microwave pinged. I took the apple pie and custard out of it.

My mum closed up her umbrella and took her raincoat off. Underneath it, she was wearing a little strappy sundress. I hadn't noticed that she'd been wearing that earlier. But, then again, she always wears summer clothes when she's popping over to A Tan for All Seasons. She reckons it helps her get into the tanning mood. As she walked through the cafe, she almost looked like Cameron Diaz. Just a slightly more knackered version.

My mum said, 'Where's Jolene? Skiving off again?' And then she looked at Liam and said, 'And who's this handsome feller? A new friend?'

Cameron Diaz might have the edge on my mum when it comes to looks but I doubt she could beat my mum in a competitive cringe-off.

'Don't be daft,' I snapped. 'He's just some random customer who came in to collect his stupid phone. Jolene's gone to get it for him.' And then I sploshed tea into a mug, picked up the molten hot bowl of apple pie and custard and got out of the way before my mum could say anything worse.

As I was putting WBH's stuff down in front of him, I heard my mum say to Liam, 'I must apologize to you, sweetheart. My children have got shocking manners. I don't know where I've gone wrong with them, I honestly don't. And what's your name, my lovely?'

And, unsurprisingly, I heard him say, 'Liam.' But he must have had a bit of dust trapped in his throat or something because he didn't sound as cool as he did before and his voice had gone all croaky.

'And you left your phone here, did you, darling?'

Liam just made another croaking noise.

'Well, Jolene certainly seems to be taking her time,' said

my mum. 'Can I get you a drink of anything while you're waiting, sugarplum?'

And Liam croaked, 'Yes, please. Can I have a smoothie?'

'With strawberries and banana?'

'Yes, please,' croaked Liam again.

I picked up Vee and Doreen's empty plates and carried them over to the sink. They'd moved on from discussing childbirth and trapdoors, and were now noisily debating which member of Take That they liked the best.

I heard Doreen say, 'For me, Vee, it's that little Mark Owen every single time. He's got the face of an angel sent down to us from heaven.'

Vee said, 'Oh no. Not him, Dor! He's addicted to nookie! I'd choose chubby Gary Barlow any day. He's much more wholesome and there's more of him to get hold of.'

And then they both started cackling into their jam roly-poly puddings.

As I passed Liam Mackie, I noticed that his face had gone massively red and he was looking a bit uncomfortable. I hesitated. Then I said, 'Are you OK?'

He nodded.

I smiled and said, 'You don't say much, do you?'

My mum put a smoothie down in front of Liam. 'There you go, handsome,' she said. 'Get your kissing gear around that.'

Liam's face went even redder. For a moment, I wondered if he was actually in the process of mutating into a tomato or something – but then I remembered something vitally important. It explained everything.

'Uh-oh,' I said to my mum. 'You've put yoghurt in his smoothie. He doesn't like it with yoghurt in.' I looked at Liam and added, 'Do you?'

Liam croaked, 'No . . . I mean yes . . . I mean I love yoghurt.' And then he downed the whole thing in one long, slow gulp. My mouth fell open in utter disbelief. Some people change their likes and dislikes just as regularly as they change their undies.

But then I pushed that thought right out of my head because any contemplation of Liam's undies was definitely a serious no-go area.

Just then, Jolene came back. She had a face like a trodden-on teacake. She put Liam's phone down on the counter, slid it over to him and said, 'Bye then. Have a nice life.'

My mum looked at Jolene and said, 'Hi, baby.' And then she frowned and said, 'Why haven't you got any trousers on?'

Jolene opened her mouth to answer.

My mum turned to Liam and said, 'Are you leaving us already, sweetheart?'

Jolene slammed her mouth shut again.

Liam croaked, 'Yes . . . I mean no.'

He seemed utterly flummoxed – which was odd really because it wasn't exactly what you'd call a difficult question. Me and my mum and Jolene stared at him. Out of the corner of my eye, I could see that my sister still had a face like a spat-out Smartie.

Liam Mackie put his phone in his pocket and scratched his head for a second. And then, suddenly, he looked at Jolene and said, 'I'd like to see that film about the moth after all.'

Jolene looked surprised. I think I did too, to be honest. It was a helluva U-turn.

'Would you?' she asked.

'Yeah,' said Liam. 'I was just kidding around before. But I really want to see you again.'

'Same,' said Jolene. Her face had brightened up.

Liam said, 'I'll drop by and see you after school tomorrow, shall I?'

'Sure,' said Jolene. She was actually smiling now.

Liam grinned. 'Sweet!' And then he leaned over the counter and kissed my sister lightly on her cheek. Just like they do in France. And he was so cool about it that he didn't even seem to care that me and my mum were watching.

And all I could do was stand there wondering what it felt like to be kissed by him.

Jim Morrison is my favourite ever singer. I may have mentioned this before. He was also a poet. He was born on the eighth of December 1943 and his life was pretty normal and un-amazing until 1965 when he made friends with a massively talented keyboard player called Ray Manzarek. Together they formed the rock band, The Doors. A little while later, Jim and Ray found a drummer called John Densmore and a guitarist called Robby Krieger and then their band was complete. From this point onward, Jim's life stopped being un-amazing.

In 1967, The Doors released their first album and a single called 'Light My Fire'. It burned all the way up the American charts to number one. This song is totally and utterly brilliant and I often lie on my bed and listen to it on repeat. Over the next four years, The Doors released five more albums and had a total of seven Top 20 singles. I often lie on my bed and listen to all these songs too. Jim had it all. Good looks. An amazing voice. And a genius way with words. But, somewhere along the way, he totally lost control of his life and then, on the third of July 1971, he died.

He was twenty-seven years old.

Jolene can't stand The Doors, but, to be fair to her, their music isn't everybody's cup of tea. It's for people who have really good taste.

Eleven months before Jim left the planet, a little baby boy was born. He was called River Jude Phoenix and he is my favourite ever film star. I may have mentioned this before as well. His birthday was the twenty-third of August 1970 and he began acting when he was only ten years old. The first film he ever starred in was a sci-fi fantasy called *Explorers* and River played the part of a science whizz-kid called Wolfgang Müller. River was so completely brilliant that he won a Youth in Film Award for an Exceptional Performance by an Actor in a Supporting Role. Even though River was fifteen years old at the time, you'd have trouble believing it because, in this film, he actually only looks about ten.

His next films were released a year later in 1986 and they were called *Stand by Me* and *Mosquito Coast*. He won awards for his brilliant acting in both of these too. Even though River was sixteen years old when he appeared in them, you'd still find it massively hard to believe because, in both these films, he only looks about eleven. Or perhaps eleven and a half. In no way does he look sixteen.

I like these early River Phoenix films, but they're not my favourites.

In 1988, River played the part of Danny Pope in *Running on Empty*. He was nominated for an Academy Award and a Golden Globe Award, but somehow he didn't win either of them. He should have done though, because his performance was utterly mesmerizing. But in the end it doesn't really matter whether he won any stupid poncey awards or not because this film will always be my favourite. I've got it on DVD and I reckon I must have watched it at least twenty times. And the reason why it's so mesmerizing is that River was eighteen years old when he starred in it and – instead of looking ten or eleven or even eleven and a half – he looks

totally and utterly amazing

from start to finish.

When I watch him, I want to hold my head in my hands and cry.

And it doesn't get any easier because River just goes on looking totally and utterly amazing in every single second of every single film he appears in. There are seven more of them. And I've got them all on DVD and I reckon I've watched every one of them at least twenty times.

Jolene has always found this pretty weird. I know because she told me. She said, 'I don't see why you have to keep watching those same old films over and over again. They're OK for killing a couple of hours, but they're not that good. Not like *Mean Girls*.'

So I shrugged my shoulders and said, 'I find them thought-provoking.'

Jolene said, 'You're weird.' Just like it was a fact. I tried not to let it bother me though. After all, she's got that picture of Bieber on her wall.

And it's really hard not to be fascinated by River Phoenix because he had absolutely everything going for him. He really did. But then one day, in 1993, he walked into a nightclub called *The Viper Room* and he never came out of it alive.

He was just twenty-three years old.

I think it's fair to say that, like Jim Morrison, River somehow lost control too.

It happens. In all sorts of ways.

And every time I'm in the cafe I hear people singing songs about it. Like Adele who can't control the fact that she's in love with somebody who doesn't love her back. And Dolly Parton who can't stop a beautiful woman called Jolene from stealing her man away from her. And then there's that song my dad is always singing – the one by the spooky old cowboy Johnny Cash. In it, Johnny sings about how he's fallen into a ring of fire and how he can't stop himself from burning up. And, personally, I don't think we're meant to interpret Johnny's words literally because he's not actually singing about being barbecued alive or anything. It's much more symbolic than that. The ring of fire represents some colossally painful experience that Johnny is having, and, as much as he wants to get himself out of that colossally painful experience, he can't. In fact, the flames around him just keep on getting higher and higher and there's absolutely nothing he can do about it. And the most tragic thing of all is that Johnny Cash makes it very clear exactly what that colossally painful experience is.

It's love.

Because sometimes love can be a very painful thing.

And I think I've always known this – so I really should have kept my mind fixed firmly on formulas and fractions. Because when I'm solving maths problems it makes me feel like I've got everything fully under control.

But I didn't. I let my mind wander and I fell in love, and this time it wasn't with an impossible unreachable face on a poster or on a television screen. It was with Liam Mackie. And, to be honest, it felt pretty much as if I'd fallen head first into a burning ring of fire.

Because I honestly never wanted to fall in love with him. In fact, I did everything I could to stop it from happening. But, however much cold water I poured over my feelings, it wasn't enough. Those flames just kept on getting higher and higher. And I definitely never meant to mess things up between Liam and my sister. I honestly didn't. And I swear to God that I didn't ever intend to be all on my own with him inside my bedroom.

It just happened.

And it happened like this.

It was the following Sunday. I'd just lived through five more colossally confusing days and Jolene and Liam had been going out together for almost a week.

Except that, technically, I don't even know if they *had* been. Because not a lot of *going out* was going on. Mostly they just *stayed in* the cafe and got on my nerves.

And, although I wasn't exactly standing behind the counter and studying their every move, it was easy enough to spot that their 'dates' pretty much followed this pattern.

1.   Liam rocks up at the cafe at around 5 p.m.
2.   Jolene instantly starts pouting poutrageously.
3.   Liam kisses her lightly on the cheek just as if he's a French person in a foreign film.
4.   Liam smiles and says hello to me and then talks in a charming manner to my mum as she makes him a strawberry and banana smoothie – with yoghurt.
5.   Jolene asks Liam if he wants to go clubbing/to the cinema/to the park/to Brent Cross Shopping Centre with her.
6.   Liam says no because he's got family visiting him/he's grounded/he has loads of coursework to do/he's all out of cash.
7.   Jolene looks disappointed.
8.   Liam kisses her full on the lips.
9.   Jolene looks very pleased.

10. They sit down together and share a deeply romantic plate of turkey twizzlers and oven chips and lean across the table every now and again to kiss a bit more.
11. I start feeling sick.
12. After a while, Liam stands up, smiles at me and says bye, and then smiles at my mum and says bye to her too.
13. My mum tells Liam he's a sweetheart and that he must call round again.
14. Liam gets embarrassed and goes all twitchy.
15. Liam goes home.
16. Jolene strops about with a face like a pickled egg and then disappears up the stairs to her bedroom.

This exact same routine happened Tuesday, Wednesday, Thursday and Friday.

Now, I'm no expert on these matters but this doesn't sound like the right pattern on which to build a successful relationship. In fact, I'm not at all sure that there is a right pattern. Don't get me wrong – patterns are incredibly useful and necessary at places like Dollis Hill tube station or Willesden Green bus terminal or Heathrow airport but we can't rely on them all the flipping time.

Because sometimes a bit of random behaviour is simply a symptom of being crazy in love.

(Beyoncé Knowles would totally understand what I'm trying to say.)

And while Jolene was acting weirdly enough and dippily enough to suggest that she possibly *might* have been in love, I don't think that Liam was at all. Not even slightly. He just seemed to be going through the motions and following the flowchart.

And then, on Saturday, he finally took her out. But it wasn't to go clubbing or to the cinema or to the park or Brent Cross Shopping Centre or to anywhere she actually wanted to go – it was to Loftus Road to watch Queens Park Rangers play Norwich City. And the worst thing of all was that Spurs were playing at home against Manchester United at the exact same time, and even though my dad had offered to buy her a ticket, Jolene had to put on her stripy socks and pretend to be a QPR fan.

'You know what, Jody,' she said, just before Liam came to call for her. 'I've got to laugh about this situation or else I'd cry an entire flipping river.'

And if you think my twin sister was stretching a point and incapable of crying quite this much I can tell you, for sure, that she wasn't. She can cry an entire flipping river. And I know because I was right on the verge of seeing it happen.

It all kicked off the next day. Sunday. Jolene was doing a shift in the cafe and I had the day off. But I was in the cafe anyway. It was raining outside and I didn't really have anything else to do. I wasn't working though – I was eating a fried-egg sandwich and reading a book called *No one Here Gets Out Alive*. It's about the life of Jim Morrison. And for once the cafe was pretty busy. Round one table, a group of workmen were chatting away together in some totally foreign language and tucking into Champion Chunky Breakfasts with extra side orders of chips. Behind the counter, my dad was frying bacon and pouring cups of tea and looking chuffed. At another table, Whispering Bob Harris was eating apple pie and custard and looking the opposite of chuffed. I don't know why. But he mostly looks like that, to be honest, so nobody was paying him much attention. The two old ladies, Vee and Doreen, were back again for matching BOGOF chicken dinners, and Natalie Snell and Latasha Joy were drinking cherry colas and giggling together in the furthest corner from me. I stayed out of their way because I don't like them. They stayed out of my way because they don't like me back.

And then the cafe door opened and Liam walked in. He saw me sitting all on my own and waved. Unfortunately, it was at the exact same moment that I stuck my tongue out to stop some runny egg yolk dribbling down my chin.

Liam grinned, pointed to his chin and said, 'You missed a bit.'

I felt my face turn burning red hot but, with a massive effort of self-control I kept my cool anyway and said, 'Yeah, course I have!' And then I just put my head down and went right on reading.

Liam said, 'Nah, Jody. You seriously have. You wanna wipe it off cos it makes you look like a three-year-old.'

My fingers flew up to my chin and made contact with sticky egg yolk.

'Thanks,' I mumbled, and rubbed it off. I swear to God, I'm going to stop eating fried-egg sandwiches. No wonder Natalie Snell and Latasha Joy never talk to me.

Liam laughed and said, 'Mind you, you are only three, aren't you? Until the end of the month and then you'll be four. Jolene told me about your weird birthday.'

I glared into my book and said, 'Did she? That's nice.'

I wanted to kill her.

Liam laughed again and said, 'I actually think it's pretty cool. It makes you special.' And then he said, 'Where's your mum?'

'She's off today,' I said. 'My dad's here instead.'

Liam's face clouded over. 'Pity. I like your mum's smoothies the best.' And then he looked over to where Jolene was and said, 'Yeah, yeah, I'm coming over to see you now, ain't I?' And then he walked off.

I sat and stared at page forty-three of my book. I wasn't reading it though. I was thinking about what he'd just said.

It makes you special.

I couldn't get those words out of my head.

And then a voice said, 'Hey, Jody, do you wanna come down to the library with me and play on my PSP? I've got some well good new games loaded on to it.'

I looked up. Chatty Chong was standing by my table and smiling down at me. He had his big bag with him.

From the furthest corner of the cafe, Natalie Snell and Latasha Joy started giggling quite a lot louder.

'Oh, I dunno,' I said. 'I really want to read my book.'

As excuses go, it was a pretty lame one. I don't blame Chatty Chong for being offended.

Chatty Chong's eyebrows rose. 'What's up?'

'Nothing,' I said.

Chatty looked at the floor. Then he looked at me again and said, 'Something's up. I ain't hardly spoke to you all week, yeah?'

My fingers fidgeted with the edges of my pages. I sort of smiled at him and sort of didn't smile and said, 'Well, you hardly talk to me all that much anyway. You hardly talk to anyone. That's why everyone calls you Chatty Chong!'

Chatty Chong's eyebrows edged up some more. He looked a bit bothered. 'Yeah, but I just talk to the people I want to, don't I?' Then he stopped looking bothered and looked a bit hopeful and said, 'I've got this amazing new maths game you should have a go at. It's called Indiana Jones and the Homogenous System of Equations.'

Natalie Snell snorted cherry cola all over the table. And all of a sudden something snapped in my head. Before I could stop myself, I said, 'Do I look like I want to play a stupid gay game?'

Chatty Chong said, 'Huh?'

From the furthest corner of the cafe, Latasha Joy – who thinks she's it just because she's got hulking great big bazookas – called out, 'Is that a private conversation about maths or can anyone join in?'

From the counter, I heard Liam laugh and say, 'Rock and Roll!'

And I know it's totally tight of me and completely and utterly unforgivably crap, but I just wanted Chatty Chong to go right away. Anywhere. Just so long as it wasn't near me.

'For God's sake, Chung Chong,' I said. 'You're such a geek, do you know that?'

Chatty Chong looked at me in shock. I'd like to think it was because someone had used his actual proper name for once, but I know that it wasn't. The reason why he was shocked and appalled was because I'd just been blatantly very nasty. I'm not proud of it.

He said, 'Thanks.' And then he picked up his big bag and walked out of the cafe.

Natalie Snell and Latasha Joy laughed and turned their attention back to their cherry colas.

Liam Mackie called out, 'Just say it how it is, Jody!'

I picked up my book and held it so that it was hiding my face. I wasn't reading it though. I was thinking about Chatty Chong and how upset he'd looked. Because of the stupid, nasty, crappy thing that *I* had said.

Liam said, 'Is that a book about Jim Morrison?' And then he came and sat down at my table.

Jolene wailed, 'Liam, stay here and talk to me.'

Liam laughed and said, 'I wanna talk to Jody. You should be working anyway!'

And then my dad laughed too and shouted, 'Well said, young man.' After that, he prodded his bacon with a fish-slice and started singing, 'And it burns . . . burns . . . burns . . .'

I continued to stare at my book. But then, after a second, I peeped over the top of it and saw that Jolene was buttering bread at the counter and giving me full-on evils. For a second, I felt a bit bad about her too and then I remembered she'd told Liam I was technically only three and stopped feeling bad. I narrowed my eyes and gave her full-on evils back.

Liam said, 'I love Jim Morrison. He was the Lizard King!'

My mouth twitched into a grin. And then I lowered my book and said, 'Rock and Roll!'

Liam smiled back at me and it was the brightest most perfect smile I've ever seen. He leaned forward across the table towards me. What's your favourite track?'

'"Light My Fire",' I said. I didn't even hesitate.

Liam's eyes grew rounder. 'Mine too,' he said. 'Although I really love that song "Touch Me" as well. It's amazing.'

I closed my book and put it on the table. 'I've got every album The Doors ever made,' I said. 'Except for the ones they did after Jim died. I can't be bothered with those.'

Liam nodded in agreement. 'Wow, I'm seriously impressed!' And then he said, 'I've only got their *Greatest Hits*.'

I almost stopped breathing. Liam Mackie was seriously impressed. With me.

Liam said, 'Can we go and listen to them?'

I stared at him. My brain was having difficulty processing what my ears had just heard. Finally I said, 'What, *now*?'

Liam shrugged. 'Why not? Jolene's working anyway. And it's busy down here. I'm just taking up space.'

'OK then,' I said. Just like that. OK then.

Liam stood up and called over to Jolene, 'I'm going upstairs for a bit with Jody. We're going to listen to The Doors.'

Jolene slapped butter on to a slice of bread and said, 'How fantastic for you both!' And then she glared at me so hard that I thought her eyeballs might burst.

My dad said, 'Chill out, Loopy Lou. Sulky Sue'll look after him. And I've got a lovely load of onions for you to chop up.' And then he laughed again and went back to singing the 'Ring of Fire' song.

Jolene said, 'Lucky, lucky me!'

In the furthest corner of the cafe, Natalie Snell and Latasha Joy started giggling again. Natalie Snell called out, 'Can we come up too?'

'No,' I said. Jolene stopped glaring at me and glared at them instead. It was a relief, to be honest.

And then, just like I was watching myself act in a very weird film, I saw myself walking up the stairs to our maisonette and Liam Mackie was one step behind me. Except that what made it even weirder was that it was actually happening.

And the next thing I knew we were sitting on my bed and listening to The Doors. 'Touch Me' was playing.

'Wow! Nice room,' said Liam. 'Your posters are cool. Jolene has got Justin Bieber on her wall.'

'I know,' I said.

'I'm not sure about your prime-number chart though,' said Liam.

'*I* like it,' I said.

Liam smiled. 'Fair dos.' And then he pointed to a picture of River Phoenix and said, 'Who's this geezer?'

'River Phoenix,' I said. 'He was an actor. But he died.'

Liam looked at River and then he looked at me. There was a cheeky sparkle in his eye. 'Do you fancy him? You've got enough pictures of him.'

'He was a good actor and I like his films,' I said. 'I find them thought-provoking.'

Liam said, 'Weird!' And then he turned his head to take another look at River. I felt like my life was being examined under a microscope. Liam laughed and said, 'His hair is well sexy!' And then he laughed again and said, 'Do you think he looks a bit like me?'

I forced my mouth into a grin. 'You reckon?' And then I went quiet because I didn't really know what else to say for the best.

Liam stood up and walked over to the window. For a moment he was still, just looking out over Willesden, and then he leaned forward and pressed his face up against the glass. 'You can see the Wembley arch from here.'

'I know,' I said.

'It looks like the big loop on a massive roller coaster or something.'

I smiled. I'd never thought of it that way. 'I think it looks like the handle on a giant's shopping basket,' I said.

Liam laughed. And then he said, 'I don't really like shopping.'

'Me neither,' I said. 'Well, not much anyway.'

For a moment we both went quiet and then Liam said, 'There's a Doors tribute band playing in Kilburn in a couple of weeks. A group of us are going. You can come along if you like.'

'I don't know,' I said. 'Maybe.'

'They're good,' said Liam. 'I've seen them before. They're called The Replacement Doors. I'll leave you my number. Give me a bell if you fancy it.'

He picked up a pencil from my desk, scribbled his phone number on to a corner of my maths project and then tore it off and handed it to me. I folded it very carefully and put it in the pocket of my jeans. I didn't even care that I'd have to draw that entire page of isosceles triangles all over again.

Liam sat back down on my bed. And then he closed his eyes and began to sing along with the track that was playing.

I hung my head and looked at my hi-tops.

Next to me, Liam went on gently singing. He was singing 'Touch Me'. He had a really nice voice.

Even though I was trying very hard not to, I turned my head and looked at him. I couldn't stop myself. And then I breathed out a big silent sigh. He had a really nice face too. But I think I've mentioned that before. A really seriously very beautiful face. I'd actually say it looked like the face of someone I'd been waiting my entire life to meet.

Just looking at him made me want to hold my head in my hands and cry.

Liam continued to sing.

I felt my heart thump inside my body. The sound of my own blood pumping past my ears was so incredibly loud that I don't think I could even hear the music any more. And then, without stopping to think about what I was doing, I did a seriously uncontrolled and random thing.

I leaned forward, brought my lips right up to Liam's lips and kissed him.

Just like that.

And, just like that, Liam's eyes flicked open and the next thing I knew there was a burning, burning, burning ring of fire all round my right eye.

Liam Mackie had hit me in the face.

Then he pushed me away from him, leaped up from my bed and said . . .

'What the hell was that? You gay piece of shit.'

For a second or two, I didn't move. I couldn't. I was

completely frozen. I just lay there, sprawled across my bed with my hand held against my throbbing eye. And then I blinked back a horrified tear and whispered, 'I'm sorry. I'm really ever so sorry. I wasn't thinking.'

And I wasn't, was I? Because why on earth did I think that Liam Mackie might actually kiss me back?

Me.

Stupid, boring, maths-loving Jody Barton.

Jody John Christopher Barton.

WHEN YOU'RE STRANGE

'Do that again and I'll mess you up.'

The violence in his voice made me flinch. But he needn't have bothered with the warning. He'd messed me up already.

'I'm sorry,' I whispered. 'It was a mistake.'

My own voice sounded weird and alien. I don't tend to whisper all that often. And I don't tend to say sorry all that often either. To be honest, I hardly ever get into trouble so I don't tend to need to.

'Too right it was,' said Liam. 'BIG mistake!'

Without moving any other part of my body a single millimetre, I shifted my eyes and dared a glance in his direction. He was standing by my bedroom door and rubbing his mouth furiously against his sleeve. Just like he was trying to wipe the taste of something terrible from his lips. Behind his arm, I could see that his face was twisted into an angry scowl and he was staring at me with eyes as hard as conkers. He still looked incredible. And he always will, I suppose. But he didn't look beautiful any more. He looked dangerous.

Liam lowered his arm and said, 'Quit staring at me!'

I let my gaze fall and looked back down at my hi-tops.

Liam said, 'Do I honestly look like a gay boy?'

'Oh God,' I said. I was still whispering. Anything louder seemed completely impossible because all the energy had disappeared right out of my body. I felt as if I'd turned into my own shadow. In fact, I might have felt less terrible if I *had*. 'Just leave it,' I muttered. 'I *said* I'm sorry.' And then I slumped forward and held my head in my hands.

Liam said, 'Do I look like a gay?'

I lifted my head up again. Using all the self-control that I could pull together, I said, 'Just keep it down a bit, will you? Someone might hear.'

Liam sneered. 'What's up, Jody? Don't you want the world to know what you are?'

'No,' I said. 'I mean . . . I dunno . . . Oh, just shut up!' I dropped my head back down into my hands and pressed my thumbs over my ears.

I could still hear him though. He said, 'You're *bent*. They'll find out sooner or later.' And then he hawked up a load of phlegm, gobbed on my bedroom carpet and left.

For a moment or so, I didn't move. I just sat there on my bed, as still as a statue, and stared down at my carpet.

Stared down at the billion bubbles of Liam Mackie's filthy frothy blob of gob.

But even though I looked like a lump of stone, my insides were wobbling around like jelly and my brain was busier than Piccadilly Circus. I could hear Liam's feet thumping down the stairs. I could hear my blood pumping in my ears. I could feel my heart pounding against my ribs. I could feel my right eye socket throbbing from where he'd decked me. And all of a sudden, amongst all this noise and confusion, I started to feel something else too. It wasn't a new feeling exactly. I'd felt it before, but only ever in manageable doses. Like when I was ten and Jolene tried to convince the classroom helper that I was adopted. Or when I was twelve and Natalie Snell stole my maths book and helped herself to my homework. Or the time in Year 9 when Mr Leonard, my PE teacher, made me do fifty press-ups in the mud just because I'd forgotten my crappy kit. Or that first time I looked up and saw Liam Mackie's face . . .

I started to feel that life was really really unfair.

And I wasn't feeling this in any manageable kind of way. I was actually feeling it in a really hard-to-handle and way-beyond-reasonable kind of way. In fact, now I come to think of it, I'd never before been struck quite so squarely by how stinkingly unfair life can sometimes be.

Because Liam Mackie was NOT the perfect and beautiful person that I'd thought he was.

And I'd tried to *kiss* him.

I lifted my arm and slowly began to wipe my mouth against the sleeve of my hoodie. And then, without really being aware of what I was doing, I stopped wiping my mouth slowly and began to wipe it really really hard and fast, and I only stopped when I realized that my lips were starting to hurt almost as much as my right eye. Letting my arm fall, I hung my head and stared back down at the floor. Liam Mackie's blob of gob sneered back up at me. And, seeing it there, foaming like a sick slug on my clean beige carpet had an instant and powerful effect on me. Every single emotion that had been whirling around in my head disappeared immediately and got replaced instead by a big, intense cloud of choking smoking rage.

'YOU TOTAL MORON,' I said. Actually, I think I may have shouted it – I was way beyond caring whether anyone downstairs would overhear. I stood up and stomped off to the bathroom. With the door locked, I examined the damage in the mirror. It was pretty bad. The area around my right eye was already so puffed up and purple that I almost didn't recognize myself. For a second, my rage vanished and I felt nothing at all but numb shock.

'Oh my God,' I said.

I raised my hand and carefully pressed my fingertips against my alien face. It felt completely the wrong shape. It also hurt like hell.

'Oh my God,' I said.

I tipped the toothbrushes into the basin, shoved the empty toothbrush glass under the tap, stomped back to my bedroom and chucked water over the gob on my carpet.

And then I threw the glass at the wall. But it didn't break because it's made out of plastic.

So I picked up the nearest thing I could lay my hands on and threw that at the wall instead. It was my scientific calculator. I only got it last year. It's plastic too but it hit the wall with a loud crack, the back snapped off and the batteries fell out.

'YOU TOTAL AND *UTTER* DICKHEAD,' I said, and grabbing hold of the end of my duvet, I pulled it right off my bed and on to the floor. And when I'd done that, I lifted up my mattress and heaved that on to the floor as well.

There was no logical reason for doing any of this. I just felt like it. And my hands were shaking so badly that I needed to give them something to do. The truth is that I was angrier than I've ever been in my entire life.

Angry with Liam for thumping me in the face.

Angry with him for flobbing on my carpet.

Angry with him for looking like River Phoenix.

I wiped my eyes on the sleeve of my hoodie again and looked around my room. River Phoenix was everywhere. And I mean everywhere. He was on colour posters I'd bought from Kilburn Market. On black and white postcards I'd picked up in Willesden Green bookshop. On pages I'd ripped out of magazines. Sometimes he was a big facial close-up and other times he was a small frozen image from a film. He was wearing sunglasses and he wasn't wearing sunglasses. He was long-lank-haired and he was sporting a big back-combed quiff. Occasionally he was smiling shyly, but mostly he was frowning intensely. And always . . . always . . . he looked utterly amazing.

And, all of a sudden, I stopped wasting my energy on being angry with Liam Mackie and began to feel really colossally furious with River Phoenix instead.

For being so beautiful.

Only – being a boy – I wasn't supposed to notice that, was I.

'This is all your stupid fault,' I said, and springing to my feet I took hold of the edges of the picture closest to me and tore it right off the wall. It was the one where River is wearing a red jacket and red trousers and a big pair of boots, and he's walking straight down the middle of this empty desert road just like he's the loneliest person in the entire world.

I crumpled the poster into a tight ball and threw it on to the floor. And then I moved on to the next picture which was a head-and-shoulders shot of River doing nothing at all other than looking impossibly handsome. I

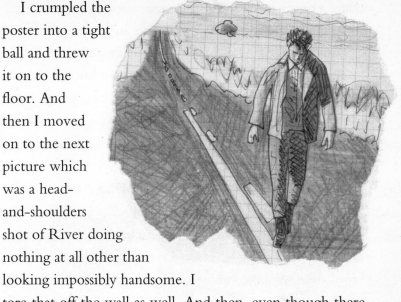

tore that off the wall as well. And then, even though there was some part of me that didn't really want to, I just carried on pulling posters and postcards and magazine clippings off my walls until there wasn't one single picture of River Phoenix left. I trashed them all. Even my original film poster of *Running on Empty* that cost me twenty-five quid and which the nice woman on Kilburn Market says is quite hard to get hold of these days.

And then I just stood there, all out of breath, and stared at my walls. They were much barer than they'd been before. For the first time in ages, I could see the Tottenham Hotspur wallpaper which my dad put up for me when I was nine and which I'd never actually asked for or wanted. My bedroom looked weird. If it hadn't been for my posters of The Doors and my prime numbers wall-chart, I might have believed that I'd wandered into a total stranger's room by mistake.

I looked at The Doors.

Three forgettable-looking blokes and Jim Morrison. No one could ever describe Jim Morrison as forgettable-looking.

And it was only then that I realized that music was still pumping out of my mega-bass super-woofer and that The Doors were still playing. Liam's favourite track had finished ages ago and now Jim was singing a song about how weird and unfriendly the world is when you're different from everyone else. For a moment, it caught me by surprise. So much other stuff had been going on that I suppose my ears had temporarily tuned out. But now that they'd tuned back in again I didn't want to listen to The Doors. In fact, they were the last band on earth I wanted to hear. Because, all of a sudden, I couldn't be certain whether it was the songs I liked or just the guy who was singing them.

As quick as I could, I reached down for the plug of my mega-bass super-woofer and yanked it out of the socket. The last thing I heard before the music abruptly cut off was the word strange.

'Yeah, you can shut right up,' I said. And then, just because I was on some sort of poster-trashing mission, I tore down every picture of Jim Morrison as well.

When I'd done, my room looked barer than ever. There was only my chart of prime numbers left. I sat down on the bare mattress-less frame of my bed and looked at it.

It was a dumb thing to have on my wall really because it only listed the prime numbers up as far as one hundred and I learned all of those off by heart yonks ago. In fact, I know all the prime numbers up as far as one thousand so I'm not entirely sure *why* the chart was still there. Other than because I really like prime numbers.

'Stupid chart,' I said, and I ripped that down as well.

Then I just sank down on to the floor of my strange Tottenham Hotspur-themed bedroom and I didn't move for about an hour. But even though I was finally acting all calm and not throwing things around and trashing stuff, there was still a whole heap of anger screwed up tight inside me. And I wasn't keeping it there for Liam Mackie or River Phoenix or for Jim Morrison or for any poor old defenceless prime number. I was keeping it there all for my stupid boy-kissing self.

MILLION POUND QUESTIONS

'Jody, can I come in?'

The knock on my door and the question that came with it made me scramble to my feet. It was my mum, fresh from the nail bar or the tanning salon or wherever it was this time that she'd been making herself look totally tanfastic. I'd forgotten about her. But, then again, I'd forgotten about my dad too. And the cafe downstairs. And the noisy High Road on the other side of my bedroom window. To be honest, I'd pretty much forgotten about the rest of Willesden Green and the entire city of London and the whole of Planet Earth in general. For all I knew, I could have been living on my own inside a giant space bubble. And that should have been OK. Because how complicated can life be if you're living on your own inside a space bubble?

Except that I *wasn't* on my own. There were two other people floating around in there with me.

Jolene and Liam.

And they both hated my guts.

'Jody, sweetheart, I need a chat.'

'Er . . .' I said. I looked around my room. It looked like I'd tried to trap a troll in there. 'Er . . . I'm a bit busy at the moment.'

'Playing on your Xbox isn't *busy*,' said my mum. 'I wouldn't ask if it wasn't important.'

'I'm not on my Xbox,' I said. 'It isn't even switched on.'

'Jody, sweetheart, I'm not gonna stand here talking to a blinking door. I just want a couple of minutes of your time.'

'All right . . . Give me one second.' I heaved my mattress back on to my bed and glanced around my room. It still looked as if I'd tried to keep King Kong captive in there.

On the other side of the door, my mum said, 'What the dibble are you doing?'

'Tidying up.'

I don't think she was expecting me to say this because she went strangely silent for a second and then she said, 'Blimey, Jode! I'll get the Hoover from the cupboard and you can give the carpet a going-over while you're at it.'

Seizing my opportunity, I scanned the room again. I was feeling desperate. In fact, I was feeling so incredibly and hopelessly desperate that it made my heart and my head and even my hair hurt. And the worst thing was that I knew I was never going to find what I was looking for – a miracle cure for my messed-up face.

Then my eyes came to rest on something almost as good as that. Untouched and untrashed on top of the wardrobe, I spotted my wi-fi gaming helmet.

My mum's footsteps were returning from the cupboard across the hallway and the dodgy wheels of our ancient vacuum cleaner were squeaking along the carpet behind her. It sounded like she was being chased by a herd of guinea pigs. As quick as I could, I reached upward, whacked the helmet on to my head and then flopped down on my duvet which was still in an untidy heap on my bedroom floor.

My mum poked her head round the edge of the door. And then she said, 'I knew you were on that bloody Xbox.'

'Sorry,' I said. My voice was a bit muffled. My wi-fi gaming helmet isn't designed for having conversations with people who are in the same building. Not unless they're both connected via the internet.

My mum looked at me and said, 'Aren't you going to take that ridiculous thing off?' And then, before I could even *try* to reply, she said, 'What on earth have you been doing in here?'

'I've been tidying up,' I said. I had to say it really carefully so that my face didn't move too much because the helmet was a bit tight and my puffy cheekbone was hurting like hell.

My mum stood in my doorway and gazed open-mouthed at the scene of devastation. I sat on my duvet on the floor and waited. I knew she wouldn't believe me. To be fair, who would?

After a moment, she nodded slowly and said, 'I suppose those posters were getting a bit tatty. Making room for some nice new ones are you, sweetheart?'

I hadn't expected her to say this. I was so surprised that I couldn't think of a single thing to say back to her. And then I said, 'Nah. I think I'll just stick with the Spurs wallpaper.'

The look of shock flashed back over my mum's face. But then she smiled and said, 'Oh, well, your dad will be chuffed. It's always bothered him that you haven't shown more interest in those boys.'

Inside my helmet, I felt my face go hot. It hurt.

My mum said, 'I'd rather you didn't pull your duvet on to the floor though, Jody. It'll get dusty. I only put a clean cover on it last week. And look . . .' She paused to wave a pointy fingernail at the wet patch on my floor. 'You've already spilt something on your carpet. I don't want you spilling drinks over your bedding too.'

'Sorry,' I said again. And I stood up and carefully arranged the duvet on the bed. But maybe I shouldn't have done because the second I'd finished and parked myself down on top of it, my mum came over and parked *her*self down on it too.

'The reason I wanted a word,' she said, 'is because your sister is a little upset.'

I stopped breathing.

My mum shook her head and sighed. 'Well, actually, she's *very* upset.'

I still didn't breathe.

'Your dad had to tell her to go and sit outside by the dustbins for a bit. She was crying so much it was depressing all the customers. He thought some wind and drizzle and the sight of a few overflowing rubbish bags might help cheer her up.'

My mum laughed a sad sort of laugh and began to fiddle with one of her hair extensions. I turned my head ever so slightly so that I could sneak a glance at her through the visor of my gaming helmet. And then, instantly, I wished I hadn't. She was frowning. And it was a big troubled frown. My mum hardly ever frowns. Most of the time she just laughs and smiles and swans around looking like Willesden Green's very own version of Cameron Diaz. Only slightly more knackered.

My head started to swim and my jaw felt heavy. I wasn't feeling too good. In fact, for one panicky second, I was so close to puking that I could taste it. Inside my helmet, I closed my eyes, swallowed hard and took a few quick deep breaths. Almost at once, the urge to barf disappeared. But I still felt awful. And I suppose that's hardly surprising really because, whichever way I looked at things, there was no escaping the obvious and uncomfortable and face-shaming truth.

I *was* awful.

I had to be. After all, the reason I was feeling so sick in the first place had pretty much nothing to do with Jolene's unhappiness and pretty much everything to do with one horrifying thought.

Liam Mackie had told her what I'd done.

I knew it. It was obvious. He'd never keep it to himself. But, then again, how much had he actually said? Had he gone into every single sad little detail – like how I'd closed my eyes and missed a heartbeat and pressed my lips up against his – or had he just said that I'd done something beyond weird? Or that I was a gayer-than-gay, back-stabbing, low-life scumbag who was not, in any way, ever to be trusted?

Not even by my own twin.

The urge to puke was back with an attitude. My fingers gripped the edge of the mattress. They had to. I might have pitched forward and fainted otherwise.

Next to me, my mum said, 'It's no good, Jody. I've got to ask you something.'

And then I knew that not only had Liam Mackie told Jolene everything, but also that Jolene had gone straight to my mum and dad and told *them* everything as well.

The whole flipping kiss and caboodle.

And now my mum was about to open her mouth and say . . .

'Are you gay?'

Three tiny words.

One massive question.

And, even though I'd spent the last week asking myself the exact same thing over and over again, I still wasn't ready with an answer. Not yet. Not now. I took a deep breath and braced myself.

My mum said, 'Will you please take that stupid thing off your head?'

I frowned. I didn't want to take it off. Even without my mashed-up face, I wasn't in the mood for eye contact.

So I said, 'Whatever it is that you want to ask me, you can ask it while I'm wearing this helmet.'

My mum said, 'Oh for Pete's sake, Jody! Just take the bloody thing off so we can have a proper chat.' And then she frowned and said, 'And what the dibble are you on about? What am I supposed to be asking you?'

I frowned. It made my face hurt. 'You just said that you wanted to ask me something.'

'*Yeah*,' said my mum. 'And I have! I asked you to take that daft crash helmet off!'

I frowned even harder. My face hurt even more, but, to be honest, I didn't care. I had other things on my mind. Relief mostly. Although, weirdly, for some reason that I can't quite explain, there was something else too. Something that felt like a quick sinking sensation of regret. But, like I said, mostly it was just pure and total relief.

'Is that *it*,' I said. I couldn't stop the amazement from flooding into my voice. '*That* was what you wanted to ask me?'

'Yeah,' said my mum. 'What's up? Should I be asking you something else?'

'No,' I said in a hurry. And then, because my face was hurting and because I'd had enough of hiding and because I suddenly really wanted that proper chat with my mum, I did something that just a few seconds earlier had seemed utterly impossible. I lifted my hands up to my helmet and pulled it off my head.

My mum smiled and said, 'Thanks, sweetheart.' And then she stopped smiling and said, 'WHAT THE DIBBLE HAVE YOU DONE TO YOUR FACE?'

I took a deep breath. 'I got into a bit of a fight.'

'You got into a *fight*?' My mum's mouth fell open. And then she took hold of my face and tried to touch my cheek with the tips of her fingers, but I backed off because it was too flipping painful.

My mum let her hand drop. She stared at me for a moment as if she couldn't quite work out who I was and then said, 'Who *with*? Who'd you get into a fight *with*?'

I hesitated. Eventually I muttered, 'Liam.'

'*Liam?*' My mum looked genuinely horrified. '*Jolene's Liam?*'

'Hm,' I said, and stared down at my hi-tops.

'*Liam did this to you?*'

'Look, it's no big deal,' I said.

My mum said, 'It is a big deal! The little thug! Look what he's done to your lovely face! You look awful. You could frighten people with a face like that.'

'All right,' I said. 'Don't go on about it.'

But my mum wasn't listening. And quite clearly she had every intention of going on about it. She took hold of my face again and said, 'Why did he hit you?'

I winced. So here we were again. Back to another million-pound question. I pulled my face away from my mum's hand, stared down at my hi-tops again and said, 'I dunno. We just . . . sort of . . . fell out.'

My mum looked at me suspiciously. 'You just *sort of fell out* and now you've got a lump the size of White Hart Lane swelling up on your face?'

I nodded.

The suspicion on my mum's face grew and she sat more upright and more uptight and folded her arms. And then she said, 'I may look like a dumb blonde to you, Jody Barton, but let me tell you something. I'm not dumb and I'm not blonde either. So why don't you tell me the truth?'

And even though it was the worst day of my whole life, I couldn't stop myself from smiling just a tiny bit. Because I've heard my mum say this a billion times before and I happen to know that it's not even her *own* rubbish joke but someone else's.

'You nicked that gag from Dolly Parton,' I said.

'Yeah, well,' said my mum with a shrug, 'Dolly is a big-hearted lady. She won't mind.'

'It's a crap gag anyway,' I said. To be honest, I was just desperately trying to change the subject.

My mum said, 'Don't try to change the subject. Tell me what this fight was about.'

I lifted my face and looked up at her. She was looking back at me with worried hazel eyes and it was like staring straight into my own eyes. And I knew then that even though I definitely didn't want to, I had to tell her the truth. Or at least something *very* close to it. Because it just doesn't seem right to tell an enormous fat lie to somebody who views the world through eyes identical to your own.

It was scary though. There were a trillion and one other ways I'd have preferred to have earned my punch in the face. Like because I'd just thrown a spectacular left hook myself or because I'd told Jolene she was crap at Call of Duty or because I'd spilt cola over Natalie Snell's gold handbag or because I'd called Liam Mackie a nasty, violent, Neanderthal moron. But there was only one reason. And, even though Liam Mackie had told me I was *bent*, there was no way that I was ever going to let him – or anyone else – call me a spineless lily-livered wimp.

Not even myself.

So there was just one thing for it. I took a deep breath and then I wedged my hands tightly under my armpits and said, 'The thing is you see, Mum . . . it's . . . complicated.' I took another deep breath. Here goes, I thought. Here goes. I opened my mouth.

My mum's hand touched my arm. Before I could say another word, she said, 'It's OK, sweetheart, you don't have to tell me. I've already worked it out.'

'You have?' I felt my face go hot. I don't know if it was with embarrassment or relief. How could my mum know? It's not as if I go *gaying* around or anything. At least, I don't think I do.

My mum smiled at me. 'You're my baby, aren't you? I know more about you than you realize.'

'Oh,' I said. 'Oh.' My face went hotter still, but this time I knew it was definitely with relief. I was so relieved that I wanted to cry. I was so relieved that I didn't even care she'd just called me *her baby*.

My mum rubbed my arm and said, 'I know you, Jody Barton. You were defending your sister's honour, weren't you?'

I froze. And then I frowned. And I thought about what had happened and how Liam had punched me in the face. And even though my face was really very boiling hot, my insides felt like one solid giant lump of ice.

My mum said, 'That little swine told you he was going to break up with Jolene, didn't he? And he said something unkind about her, didn't he? Something unnecessary?'

I opened my mouth to protest.

My mum said, 'That poor girl is out in the backyard sobbing for England. Don't tell me what he said, Jody, because I don't want to know. I'm cross enough with him as it is. And look what he's done to your lovely face! I've half a mind to ring his mother!'

'Don't do that,' I said.

My mum looked into my eyes and rubbed my arm again.

'You're a good lad, Jody. You know that? Don't you go around breaking girls' hearts, will you?'

I held my mum's gaze and didn't move. I couldn't. The slightest flicker of movement would have caused my face to crack.

My mum frowned for a second. 'That *is* what happened, isn't it?'

And because I'm such a spineless, lily-livered wimp I nodded my head and muttered, 'Yes.'

A BOY NAMED SUE

SULKY

I don't dig Johnny Cash. I know he's an American music legend who's tougher than the Terminator but I'd rather listen to anyone but him. Even Bieber. I'm not being deliberately disrespectful or anything – I'm just saying how I feel. And, anyway, it doesn't actually matter what *I* think because my dad has got the topic totally covered. He thinks Johnny is The Shizzle. So much so that he's put framed pictures of him over every wall of our cafe. To be fair, we've got framed pictures of Dolly Parton up on our walls too and, in them, Dolly is always smiling. But Johnny never is. He's always staring straight at the camera with a really mean look on his face – just as if he's daring the entire world to have a pop at him. And, to be honest, he spooks me out.

It doesn't get any better when I hear him sing. He's got

133

a voice as deep as an oil well and ten times as terrifying. It chills my blood to hear him. And on every single song he's backed by this insane crazy guitar sound which goes *boom-chicka-boom-chicka-boom-chicka-boom* . . . on and on and ON without any variation so that it sounds like a freaky great freight train is rushing right out of the stereo on a collision course with my head.

But although this stuff is annoying, it's nothing more than a surface itch. If I scratch it, it should go away. One press of the POWER button and I've got rid of him.

Except that I haven't. He's still there. Irritating the hell out of me.

And he always will be because of one Stupid Record.

The Stupid Record I'm talking about is not the one my dad is always singing. 'Ring of Fire' is actually a reasonably meaningful song when you force yourself to listen to it. But there's this other one which I really really struggle with. It does my head in every time I hear it and it does my head in even when I'm not hearing it. Johnny Cash is able to get under my skin and annoy me even when the stereo is switched off.

And it's all because of 'A Boy Named Sue.'

I think it's my least favourite song in the world.

It was playing in the cafe when I went to find Jolene.

'Go and have a chat with her,' my mum had pleaded. 'She always listens to you. It's because you're twins. I know you scrap like a couple of alley cats, but, at the end of the day, there's nothing stronger than the bond between twins, is there? You'll cheer her up. I know you will.'

I sank my chin into my hands and blew the air out of my cheeks. It made a puh sound. Just like the sound that Liam's mum had made on the phone when I'd spoken to her exactly one week before. And back then I'd felt SICK

and ANXIOUS

and EXCITED

and NERVOUS

and HAPPY

and HOPEFUL

and BUZZING

and ALIVE...

. . . because *I* was speaking to Liam Mackie's mum and because she was going to tell Liam Mackie I'd called and because Liam Mackie knew that I actually existed.

And now I just felt sick. A lot can change in a week.

But I went down to find Jolene anyway – partly just to get away from my mum. Like I said before, it isn't easy telling lies to someone who views the world through eyes identical to your own. Then again, sometimes it isn't easy telling the truth either.

Downstairs in the cafe, my dad was flipping burgers and singing along to a Johnny Cash song which he'd turned right up so that it was making the speakers rattle. It was that Stupid Record. The one I don't like. Nobody else seemed bothered by it. The old ladies, Vee and Doreen, were clapping their hands and chair-dancing and Whispering

Bob Harris was sound asleep and snoring. I looked around for Jolene, but she wasn't there. Plenty of other people were though. The crowd of foreign workmen had disappeared, but the cafe was still busy because a group of cyclists had taken their table. I could tell they were cyclists because they were wearing Lycra shorts even though it was cold enough outside to snow, and under the table were cycle helmets, water bottles and energy drinks. They were also speaking way too loudly in posh Polo-shirt voices. As I looked over, I heard one of them say, 'Crispian, should we really be eating these Champion Chunky wotyoucallits? There's so much grease on these sausages I could lube my entire bike chain.'

And Crispian, a skinny man who had a big bushy beard but hardly any essential head hair, said, 'It may look ghastly, Rufus, but we've got to keep the calories on board if we're going to manage thirty miles by sunset. Especially in this weather. Just get it down you and try not to think about it.'

I frowned and shot a quick glance back at my dad. He was still flipping his burgers and singing in a comedy voice about a boy named Sue. I was glad he hadn't heard what the cyclists had said because he's proud of his breakfasts. Suddenly annoyed, I picked up a squeezy sauce bottle from an empty table and plonked it down in the middle of them.

'There's a truckload of calories in ketchup,' I said. 'Help yourself.'

The Lycra-wearing cyclists all looked up at me to nod

their thanks. And then they caught sight of my fighter's face and quickly looked away again. For the first time since Liam punched me, I smiled. And, even though it was only a lame little smile that probably didn't even stay on my face for more than half a second, it was still a step forward. I felt different having a puffed-up purple eye. But I think I felt OK.

Just so long as nobody asked me how I got it.

'Oi, Sulky Sue,' bellowed my dad. 'What's up with your face?'

I groaned out loud. In the furthest corner of the cafe, I was aware that Natalie Snell and Latasha Joy – who'd been about to leave – had slammed themselves back down in their seats and were staring my way with open-mouthed faces of pure devil delight. I gave another inner groan. Natalie Snell shouted, 'Nice shiner, Jody. Did you have a bust-up with your calculator or somethink?'

And Latasha Joy stuck out her torpedoes and said, 'Yeah, did you and Chatty have a *lover's tiff* over who gets to use the *pertractor*?'

I felt my face sting – almost as if I'd been thumped all over again. Why was Latasha Joy dragging Chatty Chong into all of this? What had he done? What had he *ever* done? And why was she using words like *lover's tiff*? She had no right to say we'd had a *lover's tiff*! I didn't like what she was suggesting one little bit. Just like I didn't like Latasha Joy one little bit. Or Natalie Stupid Snell. They were a couple of fungus-faced miserable old hog-heads and it was high time somebody just came straight out with it and told them.

I cleared my throat. And then I muttered, 'It's not a *pertractor* – it's a protractor.'

Natalie Snell and Latasha Joy started laughing their arses off.

'Jody, get over here!'

It was my dad again. He'd turned off the stereo and was waiting for me behind the counter with his thumbs hooked into his belt-loops. I felt my heart sink. He only ever does this thumb-hooking thing when he's seriously miffed about something or when he's line-dancing. He wasn't line-dancing now. He was looking blatantly and seriously miffed. I took my quadrillionth deep breath of the day and walked over to him.

My dad unhooked one thumb, jerked it in the direction of my right eye and said, 'What's all this?'

I blew the air out of my cheeks. It made that puh sound again. And then, because I really couldn't think of anything else to say, I said, 'I dunno, Dad. But Lady Gaga is rocking this look as well so I thought I'd copy her.'

My dad didn't laugh. 'Don't be smart, sunshine. How did you get it?'

'Oh, Daaaaad,' I said. 'Do we have to go into all of this?'

'Yep,' said my dad.

'But we're in a public place,' I protested.

'Oh, don't mind us, love,' interrupted a voice from a table close by. 'We aren't listening, are we, Vee?'

My dad and I both turned. The old lady called Doreen was smiling at me with a wide-eyed look of wrinkly innocence. Meanwhile, her friend Vee had placed both her hands over her ears to show me how much she blatantly wasn't listening.

'Not a single word,' said Vee. And, then she winked and added, 'And even if we were, I can assure you that we are both the very models of discretion.'

'Yeah,' added Doreen, 'you can open up to us all you like. We aren't shocked by anything, are we, Vee? *Nothing at all!*'

And then she winked at Vee and they both started laughing their arses off even harder than Natalie Snell and Latasha Joy had done.

On the table behind them, Whispering Bob Harris suddenly twitched in his seat, opened his eyes and shouted, 'Speak up, son. I can't hear you!'

My dad put his hand on my shoulder and said, 'I tell you what, kid. We'll talk about this later.'

And even though my dad sometimes gets mistaken for a bit of a thug just because he's got a big bald head and because he's almost always wearing a Spurs football shirt and grumbling at everyone, it's the tiny little things like this which make him a legend.

'Thanks, Dad,' I muttered.

My dad looked me straight in the eye. 'I just don't want to find out that you've been up to no good.'

I held my dad's gaze and didn't move. I couldn't. The

slightest flicker of movement would have caused my face to crack.

Then he said, 'Now go and make yourself useful and have a word with your sister. She's out in the backyard being all emotional. Something to do with this Liam she's been hanging around with. I couldn't get any sense out of her at all. But you probably can. See if you can put a smile back on her face.'

'I wouldn't count on it,' I muttered, but I started to go anyway.

'Oh, and, Sulky Sue,' shouted my dad, 'no more fighting!'

I paused. And then I turned round, took a deep breath and said, 'Don't call me Sue, Dad. It really narks my nerves.'

For a split second, my dad looked surprised, but then he stopped looking surprised and started laughing his arse off.

'It's not funny,' I said. 'I'm being serious.'

My dad immediately stopped laughing and tried to look apologetic. He wasn't making a very good job of it though, because his eyes were twinkling way too much and his mouth was twitching at the corners. 'Sorry, son,' he said. 'You know I'm only trying to help. It's a rough old world out there and I'm trying to toughen you up a bit. Stop you from being a Big Girl's Blouse. And it's working innit because you're standing up for yourself. Life ain't a bed of roses for a bloke named Sulky Sue, is it?'

And then he leaned over to the stereo and pressed the POWER button, instantly filling the cafe with Johnny Cash's deep dark terrifying voice all over again.

I stood perfectly still for a moment. My heart was thumping so hard that it sounded like part of that Stupid Record.

Boom-*chicka*-boom-*chicka*-boom-*chicka*-boom.

And then, just like it was happening to someone else, I saw myself walk over to the stereo, press the EJECT button, take out the Johnny Cash CD and push it through the flap of the food-waste bin.

'Don't call me Sulky Sue,' I said. 'And never EVER call me a Big Girl's Blouse.'

My dad looked over at the bin and frowned and then he looked at me. My heart was still going boom-*chicka*-boom-*chicka*-boom-*chicka*-boom.

And, even though I wanted to turn round and run like the clappers, I stared straight at my dad and dared him to have a pop at me.

My dad's face had gone red. He looked over at the bin again and then he lifted up his hand and scratched the back of his head. Finally, after what seemed like several perishing Ice Ages, he said, 'You've just put Johnny in the rubbish bin! What the heck are you playing at?'

I swallowed hard, looked my dad right in the eye and said, 'Call me a Big Girl's Blouse ONE MORE TIME and it'll be YOU in the rubbish bin.' And then I felt sick and waited for my dad to go absolutely flipping mental.

But he just stared at me. And then he nodded. And

then – to my utter relief and bewilderment – a smile spread across his face. 'OK, son,' he said. 'Point taken. No more nicknames.'

'Good,' I whispered. It was as much as I could manage. My heart was still beating so hard that I could hardly breathe.

Still smiling, my dad raised his hand to his left eye and gave me a little salute. 'Now do me a favour, my good man, and go and sort your sister out.'

I nodded silently and turned to leave. But I hadn't even got as far as the door when I heard my dad's voice ringing out proudly above all the clatter and chatter. He was talking to those two nosy old women.

'D'you hear that? My boy is turning out to be a right proper geezer! There ain't nothing Fairy Mary about that one, thank God!'

I stood there for a second with my hand frozen on the handle of the door. And then I forced myself back to life and stumbled out of the cafe.

LOST
AT SEA

Jolene was still sitting outside by the bins. I found her sitting cross-legged on a plastic garden chair and half hidden beneath a My Little Pony sleeping bag. This wasn't a good sign. She's had that sleeping bag since she was five and, even though it's now way too small for her to actually fit inside, she still likes to hang on to it for Extreme Emotional Emergencies.

I pushed open the back door. She looked up to see who it was and then rolled her eyes and looked away. She'd clearly been crying. There were dried-up trickles of black mascara running down both her cheeks and it made her look like some scary singer in a death metal band. Even a few of her My Little Ponies now looked like they were wearing bad-ass eyeliner. I stood on the doorstep for a moment and considered doing a 180° turn. But then I forced myself forward and said, 'You all right?'

Jolene looked back at me and rolled her eyes again. 'What do you think, Sherlock?'

I put my thumbnail in my mouth and bit it. This was tricky. Not because I didn't know the answer. I did. I knew exactly what I was thinking. It was this:

How much has Liam told you?

Do you hate me?

Are you going to hate me forever?

What is Dad going to say when he finds out?

Why oh why oh why did I kiss Liam Mackie?

. . . But I wasn't prepared to share any of it. So instead I just shifted my thumbnail ever so slightly and muttered, 'Sorry.'

Jolene shivered and pulled her sleeping bag tighter. 'Yeah, well, I can do without your sympathy, thanks.' And then she frowned and said, 'What's happened to your face?'

I frowned. 'Don't you know?'

'Would I be asking if I did?'

Confused, I put my fingers up to my battered cheekbone and touched it. Even in the freezing February air, it still felt seriously sore. In fact, the swelling seemed to be getting worse. I could now actually see the fuzzy outline of my own right cheek through my slowly closing right eye. It's not a part of me that I've ever been able to look at before. Not without a mirror anyway.

Jolene said, 'So?'

I frowned again. Surely she *knew*? She *must*! Liam would have told her, wouldn't he? But, then again, maybe he *had* told her and she was just putting me through some sort of lie-detector test. Maybe it was a *twintuition* trap?

Yeah, that was it.

She was checking out my honesty.

I shut my eyes and thought about my face and what had happened to it and why it had happened. And it brought me back to that same question, which was practically glued to the inside of my eyelids.

Why did I kiss Liam Mackie?

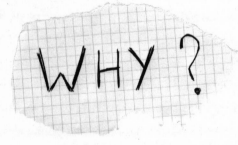

With my eyes still shut, I said, 'I don't know, Jolene. I just . . . I . . . I really don't know. I got this feeling inside and . . . I shouldn't have done it . . . but I did.'

I stood there and waited for her to start screaming.

She didn't.

For the quintillionth time, I frowned and then I tried to open my eyes but my bad eye was stuck and wouldn't budge. So, instead, I squinted at Jolene through my good eye and said, 'I'm so very sorry. I really and truly am.'

Jolene looked at me with a strange expression on her face. And then she said, 'Well that makes sense!'

'Does it?' My voice wobbled and a massive sensation of relief flooded over me. Finding someone who understands you at a time when you don't even understand yourself probably feels a lot like being pulled out of the sea by a search-and-rescue helicopter.

'Nope,' said Jolene. 'I was being sarcastic! I actually haven't got the foggiest clue what you're on about! And stop telling me you're sorry, will you? The last thing I want right now is anyone's stupid sympathy.' Then she burst into tears.

Somewhere in a parallel universe, I felt myself plunge head first from a helicopter straight into the icy depths of the Arctic Ocean.

Jolene started crying louder. I put my thumbnail back between my teeth. I hadn't heard her cry like that since The Black-Eyed Peas announced that they were having an indefinite career break. It was horrible to hear and it also made me feel as worthless as a worm.

'I'm really sorry,' I muttered.

'Stop . . . sob . . . saying . . . you're . . . sob . . . sorry,' said Jolene.

'Sorry,' I said, and then I bit my lip.

Jolene put her face in her hands and continued to cry. 'I'm not . . . sob . . . crying because I was . . . sob . . . in

love . . . sob sob sob . . . or anything. I just don't . . .
sob . . . like being . . . sob hiccup . . . dumped.'

'Ohhh,' I said, and suddenly felt slightly less like a
worm. 'That's a relief!'

Jolene dropped her hands and looked furious. 'How
exactly is that a relief?'

But before I could even answer, she added, 'I've been
humiliated, Jody! Humiliated and destroyed. And I
don't even know what I've done wrong. One second
I'm going out with Liam and the next second I'm as dumped
as a dodgy dishwasher. I've never been dumped before!
It's usually *me* that does the dumping.'

She stopped looking furious and started crying again. I
stood there feeling useless. After another minute or two,
she hiccupped a bit and sniffed a bit and said, 'Did he say
anything to you?'

I shivered. 'What do you mean?'

'While you were upstairs. Did Liam say anything about
me? Did he tell you he was going to dump me?'

'No,' I said.

'He must have said something,' said Jolene.

'No,' I mumbled. 'We didn't talk about you.' And then I
shivered again.

Jolene shook her head. 'I just don't get it. Everything was
OK until he went upstairs. And then he came down and left
without even saying bye. I tried phoning him but he'd switched
his phone off. And then a little while later I got this text.'

She fumbled about beneath her sleeping bag and pulled

out her Shame Box. After fiddling about with it for a few seconds, she handed it to me.

I looked at it.

UNKNOWN CALLER

LIAM DONT
WANNA GO
OUT WITH U
NO MORE.
TITCH

I shook my head in disbelief. 'He couldn't even tell you himself?'

'No,' said Jolene. 'I couldn't get my head round it either. So I tried calling him again and then I got *another* text.'

She waggled her fingers to get her phone back. I gave it to her. After fiddling about with it for another few seconds, she handed it to me.

I looked at it.

UNKNOWN CALLER

LIAM SAYS
STOP PHONING
HIM.
TITCH

And I continued to look at it.

Even though I'm better with numbers than I am with letters, I'm not a slow reader. If I'd wanted to, I could have handed that phone back in the time that it takes to blink.

But the truth was that I needed something to stare at. I didn't want Jolene to look me straight in the eye and see the disappointment I was feeling.

Because, only a couple of hours before, I'd thought Liam Mackie was beautiful. Properly. Perfectly. Beautiful. But, in fact, he's just a spineless, lily-livered wimp.

I don't know who I was more disappointed with. Him or myself.

Jolene said, 'I don't even know this Titch person!'

'Don't ask me,' I mumbled, and, without daring to look up, I passed the phone back to her. I was shivering pretty badly now. It can get dead cold in our backyard. Especially when you don't happen to have a My Little Pony sleeping bag wrapped round your shoulders. And, even though my mum and dad wanted me to somehow cheer Jolene up and even though I somehow wanted to tell her the God's Honest Truth, I suddenly couldn't cope with another single second of being there. The frosty air was making my eyes water and I didn't want Jolene to look at me and think I was crying. Because I wasn't. I definitely wasn't. So I did a 180° turn and began to walk to the door.

Jolene said, 'Hang on a minute. You were upstairs with Liam and now you've got a fat eye! It was Liam, wasn't it? Liam hit you!'

My body froze. But inside my head two thoughts launched into life like a rocket. They were these:

1. Here we go again!
2. TELL HER. TELL HER NOW.

With my eyes now streaming, I turned round and opened my mouth to speak. And, just as the words there's something I've got to tell you were forming on the tip of my tongue, someone else spoke. And that person said, 'How's the hero?'

It was my dad.

I quickly wiped my eyes with the back of my hand and closed my mouth.

My dad said, 'I've just been talking to your mum. She told me how you got the shiner.' And then he looked at Jolene and said, 'Your brother has been defending your honour, girl. If that QPR scumbag ever comes in my cafe again, just you let me know. I'd like to serve him up a great big piece of my mind.'

'So Liam *was* talking about me,' said Jolene.

'Oh God,' I groaned.

My dad said, 'Leave it, Jolene. Sticks 'n' stones will bruise your bones, but words will never hurt you. Not when you've got a twin brother like Jody looking out for you.' And then he clapped me on the back and said, 'You've got gravel in your guts, son. I'm proud of you. Now will the pair of you get inside before I have to drop you off down casualty and get you both checked out for hypothermia?'

Jolene looked at me. 'Thanks,' she said.

'Don't,' I said back.

'*In*,' said my dad.

We did as we were told. At the foot of the stairs, my dad said, 'I don't need you in the cafe today, Jolene. Go and play Call of Duty or something. Shoot some wrong 'uns. Cheer yourself up.' And then he punched me playfully in the shoulder and went back to his burgers.

I started to walk up the stairs.

Jolene said, 'Jode?'

I stopped.

Jolene's lip wobbled. 'Do you think everyone at school will know I've been dumped? I don't want them to. I'd rather they all think that I dumped *him*.'

I sighed. 'I don't know. But you said you didn't love him. So I don't see how it actually makes any difference.'

'Yeah,' said Jolene. 'It totally does. It makes a helluva difference to my reputation. I don't want people thinking I'm a sad dumpleton.'

I sighed again. 'Is that *seriously* all you're worried about? Whether you're a dumpleton or not?'

Jolene turned pink and looked as if she was about to cry again. With a blatantly irritated edge to her voice, she said, 'My mistake, Jody. I shouldn't expect you to understand, should I?'

I held on to the stair rail and stared at her. My eyes had started to swim again. I waited a moment or two and then, in as steady a voice as I could manage, I said, 'No, Jolene. Because I've never dumped anyone and I've never been dumped. So I don't know much really, do I? But I do know one thing for certain. Getting your reputation hammered doesn't hurt anywhere near as much as having your heart hammered.'

And I put my hand over my own battered heart and turned round and carried on walking slowly up the stairs.

AN APPOINTMENT WITH SUPERMAN

The next day, my eye wouldn't open at all and the bruise underneath it was the colour of Cherry Coke. I took one look in the mirror and decided I wasn't going to school. So I told my mum I felt sick.

She said, 'You poor pigeon! Have you been feeling peaky all night?'

And I lied and said, 'A bit, yeah.'

And she said, 'Jody, you should've come and woken me up! Do you feel dizzy as well?'

And I lied and said, 'I do a bit, yeah.'

And she said, 'Can you *see* OK? Or is your eyesight going fuzzy?'

And I think I may have got slightly carried away with the drama of it all because I said, 'Mum? What's happening?

You keep going all blurry!'

I wouldn't normally tell such a pack of pickled porkers, but I seriously did not want to go to school. Even though it was Maths Club Monday. And even though Mrs Hamood was giving us a class test on geometric sequences and I'm especially good at them. I just wanted to stay in bed and not move. And if faking an outbreak of the bubonic plague was what it took, I'd have done it.

But the problem with porkers is that they have this tendency to leave you in a worse place than where you started.

My mum said, 'Oh my good God! You've got concussion! Get dressed. I'm taking you across the road to see Dr Rash.'

'No way,' I groaned. 'We don't need to bother with that. I'll just stay in bed and I'll be as right as rain later.'

My mum said, 'Yeah, and that's what your granddad said about an hour before the angels took him. Lying in bed didn't do him any good, did it?'

'But he was ancient,' I said. 'I'm still only fifteen. Strictly speaking, I'm still only three!'

'But the twenty-ninth of February is only a couple of weeks away and then you'll be four,' said my mum. 'And, more importantly, you've got a dirty great bump on your face. So don't argue with me, Jody. Shut your pie-hole and put your clothes on.'

My mum is a difficult person to do battle with.

Fifteen minutes later, I was wearing odd socks and an

inside-out sweatshirt and standing in front of the reception desk of Dr Rash's surgery. Behind the desk was Marigold Malcolm, Senior Receptionist. Everybody knows who she is because she's built like a truck and feistier than a cage-fighter. Also, her name is printed on a badge.

'Dr Rash is off today,' snapped Marigold. 'But your son can have an appointment with the locum doctor, Dr Benjamin.'

I said, 'Ahhh no, it's not really imp—'

'Yes, please,' said my mum. Just like I wasn't even there.

'Sit down in the waiting room and Dr Benjamin will buzz Jody through when he's good and ready,' barked Marigold. 'Will you both be going into the consulting room?'

'No, she's go—'

'Yes,' said my mum.

I looked at her and frowned. And then I looked at Marigold Malcolm and frowned. And then I said, 'Err . . . Hello? I am here you know.'

Marigold looked at me. Her nostrils were flaring. 'I'll thank you not to take that tone with me, young sir. I'm just doing my job.' She sucked her cheeks in and kissed her teeth, and when she'd finished doing that she looked at my mum sympathetically and said, '*Somebody* thinks he knows it all! But they do at that age, don't they?'

My mum did a nervous little laugh and said, 'Oh, but he's a good boy really. And he can't help it. He's not even turned four yet.' She did that phony laugh again, looped her arm through mine and started to drag me off towards the rows of bolted-down chairs. My feet allowed themselves to be led away, but my eyes remained fixed on Marigold Malcolm's face. Her forehead had crumpled into a great big frown. If I wasn't so colossally fed up with the world in general, I might have found her blatant bafflement actually quite funny.

We sat down in the waiting room and started waiting. We weren't the only ones. The place was heaving. After sitting there for a while, I worked out there were five old people, four random coughers, three little children with their mums, two mismatching broken arms and me. I was at an extreme end of a sickly geometric sequence. After thinking about this for a little while, I got bored and started looking around for something new to think about. I noticed there was a small back entrance to the surgery as well as the main front entrance that we'd used on our way in. I'd never noticed this other door before.

'You don't have to stay and sit with me,' I said in a low voice. 'I'm nearly four years old after all. I'm perfectly old enough to wait by myself.'

'No, you don't,' said my mum in a low voice back to me.

'No, you don't *what*?'

My mum fiddled with her hair. 'I know you, Jody Barton. You're planning on bolting through that back door the second I get up and go. That's why I'm not shifting.'

I sat there in silence for a second or two. And then I said, 'How the heck did you know that?'

My mum smiled. 'I'm your mum, aren't I? I know what

you're thinking before you even think it.'

Instantly, images of me trying to kiss Liam Mackie's symmetrically perfect lips started scrolling through my head like a film sequence.

I quickly looked down at my hi-tops and tried to think of something else. But I couldn't. It was like my brain had got jammed on that one single head-scrambling issue. I wedged my hands tightly under my armpits and, as casually as I could, I said, 'Oh yeah? What am I thinking now then?'

My mum closed her eyes and said, 'Oooh, let me see.' And then she smiled, opened them again and said, 'Call of Duty . . . your dinner . . . pretty girls . . . the usual. Am I right?'

And, even though there was nothing remotely funny about the situation, I burst out laughing anyway and said, 'You are WAY off.' I almost shouted it.

Just then a buzzer sounded and a voice that didn't belong to Dr Rash said, 'Jody Barton to Consulting Room Five, please.'

I stood up and so did my mum. 'Nope,' I said firmly. 'I'm almost sixteen. I'm going in there by myself.'

'But I want to know what he says,' said my mum. 'I need to know you're all right.'

'I'll tell you,' I said. 'And if it's complicated or if he thinks I need a brain transplant, I'll come and get you. But please treat me like a man, will you? Because I practically am one.' And then I smiled because it suddenly struck me that I'm becoming increasingly difficult to do battle with too.

My mum looked at me for a moment and didn't say anything. And then she sat back down and said, 'The *second* he mentions the brain transplant, come and get me.'

'It's a promise,' I said, and then I turned and walked up the corridor.

All my life, I've always seen the exact same doctor. From chickenpox to ear infections to the time I jumped off a high-flying swing and twisted both my ankles at once, I've only ever seen one man. Dr Rash. Dr Rash is unsmiling and old and every time I see him he smiles less and looks older. He's also got this habit of tilting his head back when he talks so that you get a really clear view of all his grey nostril hair. It's possible that Dr Rash has made me ever so slightly doctorphobic. Marigold Malcolm hasn't helped much either.

I knocked nervously on the door of Consulting Room Five and waited.

'Come in.'

I pushed open the door and walked in.

The doctor inside was nothing like Dr Rash. For starters, he was young and had a big smile on his face. And, for seconds, he was wearing a really stylish skinny-fit shirt and the kind of black-framed glasses that you buy in places like Topshop. In fact, my overall first impression of Dr Benjamin was that he looked exactly like Superman does before he's turned super.

'Come in, come in. Sit down,' he said.

I did as I was told.

'That's a nasty knock you've got there,' said Dr Benjamin, who had stopped smiling and was frowning at my face. 'Is that what's brought you here today?'

'Yep,' I said. 'My mum thinks I've got concussion.'

Dr Benjamin gave me a sympathetic smile. 'Mums do worry a lot, don't they? But it's their job to, I suppose. Have you been sick?'

'No,' I said.

'Been *feeling* sick?'

I hesitated, unsure of whether to tell the truth or not. But then I reasoned that lying to a doctor could potentially result in a hospital visit and said, 'No.'

Dr Benjamin said, 'Any black dots in front of your eyes? Floating spaceships? Fuzzy vision? Anything like that?'

I shook my head.

Dr Benjamin got up from his chair and came and stood next to me. 'Okey dokey,' he said. 'Well, that's all good news. I'm just going to have a look at that eye. Open it up as wide as you can, please.'

I did as I was told and Dr Benjamin shone a bright little torch straight into my brain. Then he said, 'A-ha . . . uh-hum . . . ohhh-kayyy.' And then he switched his torch off.

I wedged my hands under my armpits and said, 'I don't

need a brain transplant or anything, do I?'

Dr Benjamin laughed. 'I shouldn't think so. Everything is looking exactly as it ought. Fortunately, it's your face which has suffered the injury and nothing else. You can tell your mum there's really no need to worry. All this bruising and puffiness will be gone within a week.'

'Oh,' I said. 'That's good.'

Dr Benjamin returned to his desk and started typing something into his computer. 'But I'm going to give you a prescription, Jody. It's for an anti-inflammatory. Take it three times a day and it'll help get rid of that swelling. That should also help to reduce any pain you may be feeling as well.'

'OK, thanks,' I said.

Dr Benjamin printed the prescription off on his printer and passed it to me. I folded the paper up carefully and put it into the pocket of my trackies and then I wedged my hands back under my armpits.

Dr Benjamin smiled and adjusted his Clark Kent glasses. 'Was there anything else?'

I bit my lip. And then I took a deep breath and said, 'The reason I've got a black eye is because I tried to kiss someone.'

For a moment, the words hung in the air like space invaders. I don't know who was more surprised by them. Dr Benjamin or me. Probably me. Because after only a nanosecond of delay, Dr Benjamin smiled and said, 'Well, we all make mistakes, Jody. It's part of growing up.'

I said, 'Hmm. Maybe.' And then I said, 'But it was my sister's boyfriend.'

Dr Benjamin adjusted his glasses again. I could see him trying to work things out in his head.

And, because he seemed pretty safe and because I knew that I'd probably never see him again and because I'd started and I really desperately wanted to finish, I took the biggest deep breath I've ever taken and said, 'He hit me because I tried to kiss him.'

And then I breathed out slowly and frowned at the floor.

For a moment, the consulting room was silent. I just couldn't stand the suspense so I lifted my head up again and looked Dr Benjamin right in the eye.

He scratched his ear and smiled. And then he shrugged one shoulder and said, 'You're not the first person to experience these feelings and you certainly won't be the last. And nobody should ever be punching you in the face.' Opening a drawer in his desk, he rummaged around in it and pulled something out. 'Have a read of this. It might make things a little clearer.'

I looked at the leaflet he was holding out to me. It was called *Am I gay/lesbian/bisexual?* Frowning, I took it and stuffed it quickly into my pocket. I didn't want a stupid crummy leaflet. I wanted Superman to solve my problems with his superpowers.

'And you could always book an appointment to have a chat with one of our nurses if that would help.'

'Oh, no, no, it's OK,' I said.

Dr Benjamin smiled again and shrugged both his shoulders. 'So . . . was there anything else I can help you with?'

I stared at him. And in my head I was screaming . . .

What? You mean apart from that? Does there *need* to be anything else?

Dr Benjamin's smile was fixed to his face while he waited for me to speak.

I stood up. 'Nope. That's all, thanks.' And I let myself out of Consulting Room Five and went off to find my mum.

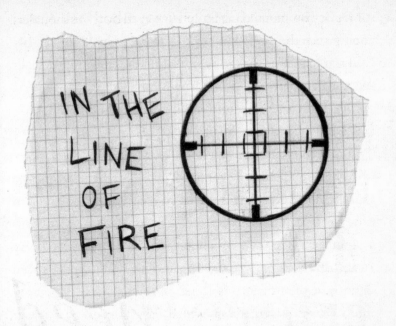

IN THE LINE OF FIRE

I spent the rest of the day in my room. I wasn't ill though. I wasn't even pretending to be ill. I was actually sitting cross-legged on a wobbly mountain of duvet and playing Call of Duty so hard that my thumbs were hurting. Strictly speaking, it's Jolene's game, not mine. I'm not really fussed on it. But, even so, there are certain days when it's handy to have it in the house. Because sometimes running around war-torn France with a submachine gun is a whole heap more preferable to staring into space and thinking about your own problems.

So I played Call of Duty for a solid two hours and fifty-three minutes and then my mum stuck her head round the door and made me lose concentration. It was almost fatal. My sergeant shouted, 'Don't stop firing,' and someone else shouted, 'Move move move,' and then an enemy grenade exploded right in front of me and sent my Damage Indicator rocketing upward. I did some secret inner swearing and pressed the PAUSE button.

My mum said, 'I hardly think you should be playing on that Xbox if you're feeling sick.'

'I'm feeling better now,' I said.

My mum raised her eyebrows. 'Well, in that case, maybe you should go back to school. If you leave now, you'll be in time for this afternoon's lessons.'

I pulled a face. 'We've got games,' I said. 'There's no way I can handle games. Not with this eye.' And then I stared intently at the frozen war scene on the telly and hoped my mum wouldn't remember which days Jolene and I dump our stinking PE kits into the laundry basket. Wednesdays and Fridays. Never Mondays.

My mum fiddled with her hair and said, 'Fair enough. But if you're well enough to participate in mindless computer violence you're well enough to go back tomorrow.'

'Fair enough,' I said. 'But it's not mindless computer violence. It's actually very deep and meaningful violence. I'm liberating France from Adolf Hitler.'

My mum said, 'Fair enough. But can I bring you a sandwich or some soup or a sausage roll or something before you liberate anyone else?'

'Fair enough,' I said. 'Can I have a ham sandwich, please?'

'Fair enough,' said my mum, and then she went away to make me one.

I unpaused the game and started wriggling forward on my belly in the direction of my next mission objective – an abandoned farmhouse that I had to make safe for the Allied forces. I didn't get very far before bullets started whizzing past my head and I was forced to take shelter behind a tree stump.

I was still sheltering there, twelve minutes later, when my bedroom door opened again. I hit the pause button, put down my controller and said, 'Ahh, thanks, Mum.' And then I immediately felt stupid because when I looked up I saw that it wasn't my mum at all. It was my dad. He was carrying a tray with a ham sandwich and a mug of tea on it.

'All right, Sulky Sue,' he said. And then he stopped dead in the doorway, closed his eyes and said, 'Sorry, son. Force of habit. Won't happen again.'

I looked at him to see if he was joking. There was no suggestion of it on his face. I flicked him an irritated glance, but decided not to make a big deal of it. He was carrying a tray with my lunch on it after all.

My dad nodded at the frozen telly screen and said, 'What you doing there, Jode? Shooting wrong 'uns?'

'I'm liberating France,' I said.

My dad nodded. 'Good for you.'

He put the tray down on my desk and gazed out of the window.

'You get a lovely view of Wembley from here,' he said.

'I know,' I said, and immediately felt my cheeks burn.

I'd had this conversation before. I probably don't need to explain when.

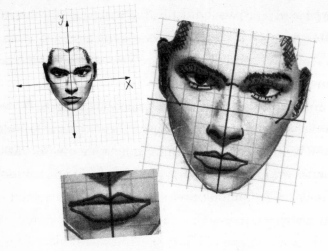

My dad said, 'So how ya diddling anyway?'

'I'm OK,' I mumbled.

My dad turned away from the window so that he could look at me. 'That was a good thing you did, Jody. Sticking up for your sister like that.'

I lowered my eyes. 'Leave it, dad,' I said in even more of a mumble, 'I didn't do anything.'

My dad shrugged. 'It's not *nothing* in my book, sunshine, but, hey, if you'd rather I didn't go on about it, I won't. Shall we talk about something else?'

'Yes please,' I said gratefully, and leaned forward to grab a sandwich.

'Spurs,' said my dad. 'Why don't we talk about Spurs?'

My fingers froze around my sandwich and my soul slipped down into my shoes. It's not that I've got any particular problem with Tottenham Hotspur. It's just like I've said before – I don't like football. When you get past all the hype and back-page headlines, there's actually nothing more going on than a load of blokes chasing after a random ball. It's not like they're liberating France from wrong 'uns or anything.

My dad nodded at my weird wallpapered walls and sat down next to me. 'Your mum told me you'd taken your posters down. She says you're gonna stick with the footy theme for a bit? I'm pleased to hear it, Jode. It was a real labour of love putting that paper up. Decorating ain't really my game.'

I smiled and said, 'Uh-huh.' And then I glanced around my bare room and felt a bit sad.

My dad said, 'Tottenham are doing well, aren't they? Is that why you're back on board?'

I nodded and said, 'Uh-huh.'

My dad laughed and cuffed me playfully round the back of the head. 'There's a name for people like you, boy.'

I looked up at him, suddenly panicked. Surely he wasn't going to start that Sulky Sue and Big Girl's Blouse thing again?

'Fair-weather supporters! You're a fair-weather supporter, ain't you? Only paying attention when your team is doing well.' And then he laughed and said, 'It don't bother me though. I'm just glad to see you showing some interest.'

I breathed out slowly and then I smiled and nodded again.

My dad grinned back at me and puffed out his cheeks. It

made that puh sound. Then he drummed his fingers on his belly for a bit and, eventually, he said, 'Gareth Bale is a good little player, ain't he? He's made all the difference down that left wing.'

I nodded and said, 'Uh-huh.' I know the name but I can't really say I'm totally sure who Gareth Bale is.

My dad said, 'It's amazing that we've made it all the way to the League Cup Final. High time we brought home some silverware for the trophy cabinet.'

'Uh-huh,' I said.

'The final is only a couple of weeks away. I've been thinking. How would you fancy coming to the match with me? You've never been to Wembley, have you?'

I looked at my dad, surprised. 'Have you got another ticket? I thought you were going with Jolene. You always take her to the football.'

My dad puffed out his cheeks again and shook his head. 'She says she doesn't want to go. Reckons she's a QPR supporter now. Reckons they've got a fancier kit. Can you believe that? A fancier kit? I ask ya! Women! They're fickle, Jody. They change their minds as often as they change their earrings. But you'll discover that for yourself soon enough.' And then he smiled and said, 'So how about I take my boy to the big match. Chunky and Son at Wembley Stadium! What do you say?'

I opened my mouth to reply, but then I closed it again. Because I couldn't speak. I honestly couldn't. It was like my dad and I were talking two completely different languages. And, even though we were sitting just centimetres apart, it suddenly seemed like we were at opposite ends of the solar system. And there weren't a million or a billion or a trillion or *even* a quadrillion miles between us. There was an entire googolplex of miles. And a googolplex is a number so BIG that it's impossible to get your brain round it.

My dad nudged me and said again, 'Chunky and Son. What do you say?'

And because I love my dad and because I didn't want to feel so scarily far apart from him, I glued a smile to my face, cuffed him playfully round the head and said, 'Sounds chuffing excellent!'

He left me alone soon after that. I ate my sandwich, ignored my mug of tea and put Call of Duty back on the box. Immediately, my sergeant shouted, 'Move move move,' so I did as I was told and ran with the rest of the men towards the abandoned farmhouse. I wasn't worried about what would happen when we got there. In fact, I was totally fearless. The return to rain-drenched, war-ravaged France was a relief. Talking to my dad had been hard work.

Keeping myself as low to the ground as I could, I edged my way forward until I had a clear view of the farmhouse. Unsurprisingly, it wasn't empty. Enemy soldiers were peeping through the open doorway and gun barrels were resting on the broken window frames. My sergeant shouted, 'Move move move,' and waved us all forward. I did as I was told and pressed on. Instantly, the enemy guns blazed into action and a shower of bullets whistled past my head. For a second, the screen turned red and my Damage Indicator flickered upward. A random voice shouted, 'Keep your head down,' so I took the advice and dived into a ditch.

But no sooner had I done that when my sergeant shouted, 'What's wrong with you? Don't stop firing!'

So I switched my view from NORMAL MODE to AIM DOWN THE SIGHT MODE, set my target on an enemy soldier and let him have the full fury of my MP40 submachine gun.

And then I watched as he toppled out of a window and pitched head first from the house.

'Ha,' I said.

'Well, that's one less to worry about,' shouted someone else.

My sergeant yelled, 'Move move move. Let's make this house safe!'

'Yeah,' I said. 'Let's damn well make this house safe!' And then I opened fire on another occupied window and caused more men to plunge head first from it. 'Got you,' I said. I think I may have been shouting a bit.

And then a really weird thing happened.

Liam Mackie gatecrashed my computer game.

He popped his head out through one of the other broken windows of the farmhouse and shouted, 'What the hell was that? You gay piece of . . .'

I didn't hear the end of his sentence because my heart was thumping so loudly that all I could hear was:

boom-*chicka*-boom-*chicka*-boom-*chicka*-boom-*chicka*-boom.

I knew how it ended though.

I squinted down the barrel of my gun and lined Liam up in the target.

But then I frowned and lowered my controller.

My sergeant shouted, 'Don't stop firing,' and somebody else shouted, 'Look out! Enemy grenade!' And, before I had time to even blink, the screen exploded into total chaos and I was suddenly looking up at the grey French sky. My Damage Indicator rocketed up to the maximum, the sky faded and everything turned red and stayed red.

I'd been hit. Fatally.

'Stupid game,' I muttered.

Mournful military music filled my room.

I did some secret inner swearing and reached forward to turn the telly off. But then I paused. Written across the screen in big letters were these words:

"AN EYE FOR AN EYE
MAKES THE WHOLE WORLD BLIND."
—MAHATMA GANDHI

I read them and then I read them again. Call of Duty always ends with some weird message like this, but I've never actually paid any attention before.

But I know who Mahatma Gandhi was. We learned about him in R.E. His real name was Mohandas Karamchand Gandhi and he was the little bald Indian feller who never wore any shoes and who waged a war against the entire might of the British Empire. And eventually he sent the British packing and gave India back to the Indian people.

And he did all this without using any violence.

Which means that he wasn't *really* a little man at all, was he? In terms of impact, he was actually a great big incredible genius of a man who'll be respected and remembered by shedloads of people forever.

The more I thought about Gandhi's words, the more they made sense. Liam Mackie hit me. He didn't have to hit me. One word and I'd have backed off faster than Lewis Hamilton driving in reverse down a ski slope. But instead he hit me and gave me a dirty great shiner just because he's got a violent and nasty streak in him. And if I went after him now and thumped him back I'd be just as violent and as nasty as him.

Not that I ever would, of course. I don't like physical confrontations. Even Jolene beats me in a fight.

I put my thumbnail in my mouth and chewed it.

I had almost pulled a trigger and blasted him to bits though. Virtually rather than *actually* – but it's the thought that counts.

'Stupid game,' I muttered, and I threw the controller down on the floor. And then I chewed my thumbnail a bit more and tried to think of something else.

But I couldn't. As much as I tried, I just couldn't shake the worrying realization that – for one dodgy second – the idea of shooting Liam Mackie had seemed perfectly reasonable. I puffed out my cheeks until they made that puh sound. Then I drummed my fingers against my belly for a bit and then, eventually, I said out loud, 'Jeez, Jody! Get a grip!'

And then I made a decision. I was going to sort this thing out. Not for me. But for Jolene and Liam. Because if I hadn't blundered in with my eyes closed and messed everything up so amazingly badly they'd probably still be sharing plates of chips and snogging each other across one of the cafe tables. All right, so Liam had punched me. He must have been shocked by what I'd done. I could hardly blame him for that. I was pretty shocked myself.

I sat on my bed for a moment or two more and then I

stood up, dug my hand into the pocket of my trackies and pulled out a couple of pieces of paper. The first, scrunched up and sad-looking, was that leaflet called *Am I gay/lesbian/bisexual?*. I scrunched it up some more and buried it in my bin.

And then I dug it out of the bin, smoothed it flat to get the creases out and put it carefully under my mattress.

The second piece of paper, folded into a neat square, was the edge of a page torn from my maths project. And it had Liam Mackie's phone number written down on it in Liam Mackie's own handwriting.

I held the scrap of paper between my hands and stared at it. Then I laid it down on my duvet, picked up my phone and keyed in the number. And even though I was as scared as a scarecrow having a panic attack, I kept on thinking about Mohandas Karamchand Gandhi and how brave and strong and big that bare-footed little man *actually* was.

Liam's phone rang a couple of times. And then he said, 'Hello?'

My mouth had gone completely dry. I grabbed the mug of cold tea from my desk, took a swig and said, 'It's Jody. Jody Barton.'

There was a long pause. And then Liam said, 'What do you want, gay boy?'

I took another swig of cold tea, but somehow I missed my mouth and most of it went down my chin. Wiping my face on my sleeve, I took a deep breath and said, 'Two things. Number One, I want to say sorry. I said it yesterday but I'm saying it again. Sorry.'

'Yeah yeah yeah,' said Liam. 'Yadder yadder yadder. What was the other thing?'

'Jolene,' I said. 'She's upset. She cried all day yesterday. And she wasn't exactly Little Miss Sunshine when she went to school this morning. You didn't have to dump her because of me, you know. I can promise you I'll stay well out of your way from now on.'

There was another long pause and then Liam started laughing. 'I didn't dump her because of *you*,' he said. 'Well . . . maybe I did . . . but I'd have dumped her anyway soon enough.'

I didn't know what to say to that. I was confused.

'I never liked her in the first place,' explained Liam.

I felt my face go hot. 'So why did you go out with her then?' I said. I think I might even have shouted it.

Liam laughed again. 'It was just an excuse to come round and see your mum. Now, she is well fit! If *she* ever wants me to take her to a film, you can tell her that I'm well up for it.'

My jaw dropped open. For a moment I was so incredibly, blood-boilingly . . .

ANGRY

. . . that I could barely breathe – let alone speak. Just for a second, Liam's face appeared in my target again.

But then I stood up straighter, lifted my chin and very calmly said, 'Stay away from my sister and stay away from my mum and don't ever come near our cafe again.' And then I pressed END CALL.

I seriously can't believe that I ever thought Liam Mackie was beautiful. He's definitely good-looking, yeah. But his beauty is about as deep as a coat of paint.

And I was still thinking about this when my phone buzzed and began to vibrate. I'd received a text message. I looked at the screen.

UNKNOWN CALLER

LETS SEE HOW HARD YOU ARE WHEN I TELL EVERYONE YOUR SECRET
:-)

I knew it was Liam. Who else would it be? And he'd made a smiley face at the end of his message to show me how much he was laughing. I stared in horror at my phone for a googolplex of lifetimes and then, aware that something was flickering on the telly, I dragged my eyes away and turned to see what was going on. Gandhi's words had disappeared. And in their place were two new ones, flashing at me like a warning light . . .

GRAND CENTRAL DESPAIR

The next morning I got up and did all the usual things. I put on my school uniform, ate two bowls of Coco Crunchies, grabbed my lunch box from the cafe and my school bag from the hallway, and followed Jolene outdoors before the earliest of my dad's hungry customers had even arrived. Just like it was any regular day.

Except that it wasn't because I had absolutely no intention of going to school.

I walked with Jolene until we reached the bus stop outside Willesden Green Tube Station and then I dumped my bag down on the pavement and said, 'I'll see you later. I'm having the day off.'

Jolene stopped too and stared at me. And then she folded her arms very tightly and said, 'What the fandango is going on with you, Jody Barton?

'Nothing,' I snapped. 'Everything's fine.' And then I felt a bit shifty and deliberately looked in another direction. I'd kissed a boy. Or tried to. I doubt that my dad would agree that everything was fine.

A double-decker bus rumbled past us and filled the air with exhaust fumes. I coughed and turned round to see the noses of Natalie Snell and Latasha Joy pressed flat against its back window. Natalie Snell had her mouth wide open and her tongue hanging out.

Jolene said, 'Look, Jody. Whatever it is that's wrong, you can tell *me*. I'm your twin, innit. You can tell me *anything*.'

Ninety-nine per cent of the time, Jolene Janine Christabel Barton is a right royal pain in the brain. But very occasionally she's niceness in a bottle with no catch attached. And the truth is that I'm closer to her than I am to anyone else in the whole wide world. So I suppose that's why I love her regardless.

I looked straight at her and said, 'Jolene, there's something I've got to tell you.'

'I knew it,' said Jolene. 'I knew there was something! Have you been running up a massive bill on Mum's iTunes account again?'

'No,' I said. 'It's nothing like that. It's a lot more compli—'

Jolene's eyes lit up. 'You've been cheating in maths, haven't you? All this time I thought you were a geeky genius, but now you're about to tell me that you're as thick as a brick and you've been copying off Chatty

Chong. You are the limit you are, Jody.'

'No,' I said. 'I've never copied off anyone in my life. I—'

'OMG, you've been caught looking at the dirty mags in Mr Mulligan's newsagents, haven't you?'

'No way,' I said. And then I shook my head and added, 'For God's sake!'

Jolene wrinkled up her face. 'It's none of those things?'

'No.' I was feeling pretty appalled.

Jolene's face wrinkled up even more. 'So what the heck is it?'

I heaved out a sigh and then I looked down at my watch. In ten minutes, we were supposed to be settling down for registration.

'I can't tell you here,' I said. 'Can we go somewhere else? How about Brent Cross Shopping Centre? We can hang around the Hollister shop and see if someone will give us their carrier bag.'

Jolene's eyes grew big and excited. 'Oooh, it smells amazing in that shop!' Then she looked all concerned again and said, 'But you promise you'll tell me what's going on, yeah?'

'Totally.'

Jolene smiled and linked her arm through mine. 'Come on then. I'm totes with you!'

We did a 90° direction shift so that we could both look out for the number 266 which passes in front of the tube station and goes to Brent Cross. But we'd not been looking for more than ten seconds before a big loud mouth further along the pavement shouted, 'HEY JOLENE, WHERE ARE YOU ROLLING?'

Jolene immediately did a 90° direction reversal.

'Oh no,' I said, and did some silent inner swearing. And then I turned too. I pretty much knew what I was about to see though.

Natalie Snell and Latasha Joy had got off the bus. They were hurrying along the pavement to join us. Well, not really *us*. Just Jolene.

Jolene flicked her fringe and turned her volume up. 'Wassup, sistas?'

Natalie and Latasha continued rushing forward until they were both about one millimetre away from Jolene's face and then stopped. Natalie opened her mouth, stuck out her tongue – which had a bit of metal sunk into it – and said, 'Check out my new piercing!' And then she said, 'So where are you rolling at? School ain't that way.'

And Latasha jiggled her jubblies and said, 'Yeah, you can't get to it on the Jubilee Line.'

I put my hands in my pockets, crossed my fingers and secretly prayed, 'Please don't tell them where we're going. Please don't tell them where we're going.'

Jolene said, 'We ain't getting on the tube. We're waiting for the bus. Bro-Jo and me are going to Brent Cross. Wanna come?'

Noooooooooo,

I secretly screamed. Publicly, I looked at Jolene, raised

my eyebrows and said, '*Bro-Jo?*'

Jolene said, 'Yeah. You're my *bro* and your name is *Jo*. So what's your beef?'

I really wish Jolene would stop speaking like she's Jay-Z every time she gets together with Snelljoy. In a very sensible voice I said, 'I don't have any beef, Jolene. But I was going to tell you something, *remember?*'

Natalie Snell said, 'Brent Cross is yesterdays though. Nowadays, everyone gets on the Jubilee Line to Bond Street and then changes to a Central Line train for Stratford and then walks to the bus stop at Angel Lane and gets on a 241 to Stratford City and then just does all their business in the bling new shopping centre at Westfield. Why are you still bothering with Brent Cross?'

And Latasha Joy said, 'Yeah, Jolene, Brent Cross is sooooooo local!'

But before my sister had a chance to reply, Natalie Snell waggled a finger in her face and said, 'That kid I was telling you about in my geography class – Tyler Smith – he's still WELL got the hots for you, ain't it?'

And Latasha Joy added, 'He's Natalie's cousin. He's proper nanging.'

Natalie Snell said, 'Are you totes one hundred per cent certain you ain't interested?'

And Latasha Joy added, 'Liam's hot, yeah? But there ain't no way he's more of a buff bomb than Nat's cousin.'

I held my breath.

Jolene reddened. 'I'm not going out with Liam any more.' Her volume had gone back down to normal.

Natalie Snell's mouth fell open so that we could both see her tongue stud again. Then she said, 'OMG! Message me!'

And Latasha Joy jabbed an invisible keypad with her index finger and said, 'Don't go through the break-up on your own, Jolene.'

I think they'd all forgotten about me. Even though there wasn't a bus coming, I pulled Jolene's sleeve and said, 'Come on, let's get going.'

But Jolene just kept on facing Natalie and Latasha and said, 'This Tyler kid. Are you gonna be seeing him today?'

Natalie Snell's eyes lit up. 'You want me to have a word?' Her volume had gone down a bit as well.

Lastasha Joy said, 'Nat and Ty are cousins. Nat can fix you up with him no bother.' *Her* volume was still cranked up to the max.

'Come on, Jolene,' I said. To my relief, I could now see the 266 making its way towards us down the road. But Jolene just kept on looking at Natalie and Latasha and said, 'I am single. And if he likes me, I'm not outright saying no I won't go out with him if I like him. If you know what I mean.'

'Of course,' said Natalie.

'Totes,' said Latasha.

I was just confused. I pulled Jolene's sleeve again, nodded towards the 266, which was pulling up beside us, and said, 'Are we going or what?'

'I can set you up with him at break-time if you like,' said Natalie.

'She can do it easy,' added Latasha, who had finally decided to ditch the shouting too.

Jolene said, 'Really? Ohmigodohmigod.' And then she turned to me and said, 'Can we have that chat later? This could be one of those life-changing moments you always hear about.'

I puffed out my cheeks until they went puh. And then I said, 'So you're not coming with me then?'

Jolene said, 'Nah. Is that OK?'

And I said, 'Right. OK. Right.' And I picked up my school bag and boarded the bus by myself.

I know it's wrong to generalize, but my dad was right about women. They change their minds as often as they change their earrings.

It was a depressing ride to Brent Cross. The bus driver might as well have been taking me to a place called Grand Central Despair because I had this hopeless feeling of looming doom every single second of the way – and even though I kept closing my eyes and thinking really hard about maths, I couldn't quite shake it. So in the end I just stared out at the grey streets of Brent and kept anxiously looking at my phone every four seconds to check that Liam Mackie hadn't sent me any more terrifying texts.

To my relief, my phone was quiet. I knew it couldn't last though.

But it did for a while. My phone stayed silent and asleep for the whole time that I hung around the Hollister shop, the whole time that I played around on the escalators and almost all the time that I sat in Super Burger and slow-drank a cup of tea. And then, just as I was getting up to go, my phone buzzed and vibrated and woke up again.

It was a message.

Without breathing, I clicked on the envelope and read it.

UNKNOWN CALLER

JUST BEEN TALKING TO YOUR SISTER. LOL! LIAM

It was really good of him to put his name at the bottom. I'd never have guessed who it was from otherwise.

I collapsed back down in my seat and put my head in my hands.

This was easily the worst mess I'd ever been in. Fermat's Last Theorem must have been a doddle compared to this.

Because I couldn't think of what to do for the best, I just sat there. And I'd probably have sat there until the whole building closed – but then a voice too close to my head said, 'Penny for your thoughts.'

I jumped and lifted my head up. The whiskery face of a very old lady was staring straight at me from a distance that was well within my personal space barrier. I jumped again and said, 'Waaarrgh!' And then I realized I knew this old lady. It was Doreen who comes into our cafe.

'Sorry, sweetheart,' she said. 'Didn't mean to scare the crap out of you. I just saw you sitting there on your own – looking like you've got the weight of the world on your shoulders – and I thought I should say something. Check you're OK. You're Chunky's boy, ain't you?'

'Mm,' I said, and started to get up.

Doreen called over to the Super Burger counter and said, 'Oi, lovey! I know you don't normally do table service but be a good lad and bring us over another cuppa, will you? And make it a nice strong one with two sugars. This boy needs a good brew.'

'Oh, no . . . really, it's OK,' I said. 'I need to be going anyway.'

'Nonsense,' said Doreen. 'You'll ruddy well do as you're told and sit down with me and Vee for a bit.' And then she waved to someone on the other side of the Super Burger eating area and I saw that Vee was sitting at another table and already pulling up a third chair so I could join them.

My heart sank. I was totally not in the mood. To be

honest, I don't think there's ever been an occasion when I might have been *in* the mood for this situation. And I don't think there ever will be. But it's not nice to argue with old ladies so I forced my mouth into the shape of a smile and politely followed Doreen over to her table.

'I can't stay long,' I said. 'I've really got to go.'

'Of course you have,' said Doreen, and looked at me over the top of her glasses. 'Because school starts in a minute, doesn't it. Or did it start about two and a half hours ago?'

I didn't say anything.

Doreen took the lid off my styrofoam cup of tea and pushed it across the table to me. 'To be honest, sweetheart, you're doing us a favour. It's not often we get to sit and talk to handsome young fellers like you any more, is it, Vee?'

Vee leaned forward. 'No, darling,' she said to me. 'Although, strictly speaking, I never really spoke to too many handsome young fellers even when I was in my prime. And Doreen definitely didn't. She always went out with right shockers.'

I smiled. I couldn't help it. They were forcing me to.

Doreen said, 'I see that cuppa tea is working its magic. There's nothing in this world that a cuppa tea can't fix. Is there, Vee?'

'Nothing,' agreed Vee. 'If they took Tony Blair and Barack Obama and the ayatollah and that tiny little Frenchman with the big heels and that hunky Russian prime minister, Vladimir Rasputin and put them altogether in my front room with a great big pot of tea and a jar of ginger hard-bakes, you'd have every single one of the world's problems sorted out by the end of the day. You mark my words!'

'But Tony Blair's not in charge any more,' I said. 'He got kicked out ages ago.'

Vee pulled her neck back and looked at me as if she totally disagreed. And then she shrugged her shoulders, sipped her tea and went into a sulk.

Doreen said, 'We've been doing a lovely spot of shopping. There's a Buy One Get One Free offer on at Miss Seventy so we both got ourselves a brand-new pair of slacks, didn't we, Vee?'

Vee nodded but didn't say anything. I think she was still cheesed off about the Tony Blair thing. I didn't say anything either because I didn't have the faintest clue what *slacks* were.

Doreen smiled at me and said, 'And what about you? What brings you here today?'

'Not much,' I said.

Doreen nodded. 'A change of scenery, is it? Sometimes a change is as good as a rest.' And then she smiled at me again and said, 'Especially when you've got the weight of the world on your bonce.'

I squeezed my styrofoam cup. 'I haven't. I'm fine. Really I am.'

Doreen patted my arm. 'Do you know who the wisest person alive in the world today is?'

'Nope,' I said. 'Do you?'

She nodded. 'Yes I do, dear. Do you want me to tell you?'

'OK,' I said. To be fair, I was genuinely quite interested.

'Oprah Winfrey,' she said. 'Ain't that right, Vee?'

Vee nodded and perked up. 'Absolutely. There's nothing Oprah couldn't help you with. If she sat down in my front room with Tony Blair and Barack Obama and the ayatollah and that little Frenchman with the big nose and Rasputin, you'd have the world's problems sorted out in no time.'

I decided not to say anything this time.

Doreen said, 'I'm a big fan of Oprah. She says a lot of sensible things. And one of those things was this.' Doreen paused, closed her eyes and clasped her hands in front of her. And then – in an American accent – she said, '*Difficulties come when you don't pay attention to life's whisper. Life always whispers to you first. But if you ignore the whisper, sooner or later you'll get a scream.*'

It was by far the freakiest thing I have ever witnessed in my whole life.

Apart from that though, the words did make sense.

Doreen opened her eyes. 'Whatever is troubling you, young man, you've got to listen to the whisper. You can't ignore it. You've got to listen to what your heart is telling you. And then somehow – by hook or by crook – you'll get through it. Ain't that right, Vee?'

Vee nodded thoughtfully. 'It certainly is, Doreen. It certainly is.'

I left them to it shortly after that. I went and sat by the fountain in the middle of the shopping centre. I kept on thinking about what Oprah Winfrey had said. She was right.

Life does whisper. I had a whisper in my head all right. I just wasn't sure if I wanted to listen to it.

And I was still thinking about all this when Jolene showed up.

Before she even said a single word, I knew she knew. And she knew I knew she knew. It was blatantly obvious all round.

Her eyes were almost as puffy as my fist-damaged one and her mascara was seriously smudged.

I blew out my cheeks until they made that puh sound and then I said, 'I'm so sorry.'

Jolene sniffed and folded her arms really tightly. And then she sat down next to me on the edge of the fountain. I didn't know what else to say so I waited for her to speak first.

A googolplex of years passed. And then she said, 'So guess what, Jody. Liam phoned me.'

I folded my arms really tightly too and looked down at my hi-tops. We're not allowed to wear hi-tops to school. When I'd put them on, the one certain thing in my head had been that I definitely wasn't going in.

Jolene said, 'It's bad enough that you hit on my boyfriend behind my back, but do you know what really upsets me?'

My hand moved up to my mouth and, for a moment, I bit my fingernails. But then I stopped and moved my hand up to cover my eyes instead. Tears had started leaking out all over the place.

Jolene said, 'I don't give a flying monkey that you're gay. But you never told me. I'm your twin sister and you never told me.'

I rubbed my eyes with the back of my hand and swallowed down the enormous lump that had grown in my throat.

'I couldn't,' I croaked. 'How could I? I'm not sure that I *am* gay. It was just *him*, that's all.'

Jolene sucked her cheeks in. 'So you're blaming Liam? It's *his* fault, is it?'

'No,' I said. 'It's not his *fault*. It's not anybody's *fault*. I just . . . liked him. *Really* liked him. I thought he was beautiful. I thought he was River Phoenix.'

And then I stopped speaking and covered my eyes up again because – however much I wanted to ignore the whispers in my heart – I realized that what I'd just said couldn't have sounded any gayer if I'd tried.

Jolene sat next to me for a moment or two and didn't move a muscle. And then she said, 'So you tried to get off with Liam and waited for *him* to tell me instead. That's nice. That's good to know. Thanks very much, Bro-Jo.'

'I'm sorry,' I said. I don't know if she heard it though. The lump in my throat was so huge that I could hardly breathe.

Jolene stood up. 'I don't care about Liam. Turns out he's a Nasty Boy, anyway. But I care about you. Or I did.' She sniffed and lifted her eyes so that they were staring straight into mine. And when she looked at me there was no fury or fire or fight, just a dull, dead look of disappointment. She sniffed again and said, 'Go and get yourself another twin, Jody.'

And then she walked away and left me sitting there.

RUNNING ON EMPTY

The library at Willesden Green is so close to our cafe that it's almost a part of it. All my life it's been there, and all my life I've breezed in and out of its big front doors and felt so totally at home that I pretty much feel like part of the furniture. In fact, that library is a bit like my own personal chill-out zone. Except that I share it with thousands of other people. And we all breeze about the rows of books and read and surf and chat and type and cough and whisper and sit and stare and doze and daydream and somehow manage to stay fairly and squarely and absolutely well and truly OUT of each other's way. So, although it's always busy, it's actually one of the most peaceful and calming places in the whole of Willesden Green. Perhaps, even, the world.

And the day after that terrible conversation with my sister

Willesden Library became more than just a place to chill out. It became the place that saved my life.

Because, until I pushed open those big double doors, I was running on empty with nowhere to go.

Basically, it was like this: I couldn't stay at home unless I faked the plague, but if I faked the plague my mum would have sent me straight back to Superman. And Superman had turned out to be a total letdown.

I couldn't sit in Gladstone Park all day because Gladstone Park in February is not the warmest place in the world to stop and sit. In fact, it's so flipping freezing that it can actually make your acorns ache.

I couldn't wander around Brent Cross Shopping Centre all day because I didn't want to see that stupid fountain ever again.

I couldn't wander around central London all day because wandering around central London is only fun with wads of wonga in your pocket and at least one friend to keep you company. When you're on your own and broke, it tends to be a bit depressing.

And I absolutely definitely could not go to school because everyone there was blabbing about what I'd done. And I knew this for a fact because they were kind enough to keep me informed.

My phone can't get the internet. It's too much of a Shame Box. But it still gets texts. And Tuesday afternoon, before I'd even made it back from Brent Cross Shopping Centre, it started getting more texts than usual.

I was still sitting by that fountain – feeling flipping terrible – when my phone buzzed.

I pulled it out of my pocket to look at it. And I saw a single word written on my screen:

Battyman

I've got no idea who typed that word and sent it to me. But I knew what it meant.

I sat by the fountain and stared at my phone until my eyeballs hurt. And then I switched it off, caught a 266 back to Willesden and went straight home to bed.

I didn't even have any tea. When my mum pushed her head round the door to tell me that tea was on the table, I told her I was on a one-day detox.

My mum looked annoyed, waved a pointy fingernail at me and said, 'Next time, would you please have the dibbling decency to inform me first?' And then she slammed my door shut and thumped off down the stairs. I suppose I'm lucky. Most mums would never have let me get away with that. But words like body-polish, full exfoliation and one-day detox hold a lot of sway with my mum.

By the next morning, I'd had another thirty-seven texts. I only opened the first two. They weren't nice either. So I switched my phone off, put my school uniform on and went to find Jolene. She was downstairs in the cafe, eating toast. My dad was getting the cafe ready for the day and peeling potatoes.

'All right, sunshine,' he said as I helped myself to a breakfast pastry. 'How's the detox going?' And then he shook his head and said, 'Detox? I ask ya! Ain't natural.' And then he kept on shaking his head and said, 'I'm making us all beef burgers tonight. I've got proper top quality mince as well and I don't want any of it wasted – so no more of your funny detox business, all right?'

'OK, keep your hair on,' I said. And then I shoved my entire pastry into my mouth because I was totally flipping starving.

My dad said, 'Will do, kiddo, will do.' And then he touched his head and said, 'OH MY DAYS! WHERE'S IT GONE!'

Unlike his top quality mince, my dad's jokes don't have a use-by date.

I took another pastry and sat down opposite Jolene.

'There are other tables,' she muttered.

I slid my phone over to her. 'I'm getting loads of texts,' I said.

Jolene said, 'Lucky you,' and then she slid the phone straight back at me and carried on chewing her toast.

'They aren't nice texts,' I said. 'And I don't know who they're from.'

'Well, don't flipping well ask me,' said Jolene. 'Why would I flipping know who texts you? I don't actually think I know anything about you.'

I didn't know what to say to that. After a moment or two, I said, 'So you haven't been giving out my number?'

Jolene's slice of toast froze in front of her face. And then she slapped it back down on her plate and said, 'For God's sake, Jody!'

My dad called over from the counter. 'Oi, no arguing in here, please. It makes the food go off.' And then he grinned and added, 'And don't forget, kids, it's both your birthdays in a couple of weeks. The big one. Sweet sixteen! Well, technically Jody is four but we won't let that be a problem.'

Jolene and I just stared at him.

My dad shrugged and said, 'Blimey. Don't get overexcited.'

Without another word, my sister stood up, took her plate over to the sink and then headed for the door. But as she passed me, she paused and hissed, 'Walk to school by yourself because I'm not walking with you.'

And I stared at the table and said, 'OK, I will.' But I'm pretty sure we both knew that I wasn't going anyway.

So I picked up my school bag, walked around the block for a bit and then snuck back to the library.

I was pretty cold by then. Walking around Willesden in February isn't the warmest thing to do in the world. I headed straight for the loos, pushed on one of the hand-dryers and sat down underneath it for a few minutes.

Once I'd warmed up, I unzipped my coat, took off my school sweatshirt and pulled out another jumper from my school bag. It was a proper actual jumper. Not a sweatshirt. Not a hoody. Not a long-sleeved T-shirt with a band name written on the front. It was a jumper. Made out of woolly stuff. With a v-neck. My mum got it for me once. I've hardly ever worn it. Because nobody ever really wears v-necks, do they? Not until they're at least twenty-seven.

I pulled the jumper over my head and looked in the mirror.

A young guy with a nasty black eye and a boring taste in knitwear stared back at me. He didn't look like Jody Barton. But, then again, he didn't look like he was skipping school either. Because skipping school is a teen thing and this guy looked way too old and too anxious to be bothering with teen stuff. Satisfied that I wasn't about to get harassed by any truancy officers, I stuffed my school sweatshirt back into my bag and went into the library.

Charity was on the desk. I know pretty much all the librarians who work in my library and they know me. Some of them are nicer than others but none of them are mean. They wouldn't dob me in to a truancy officer.

Charity said, 'Morning, Jody. Shouldn't you be somewhere?'

'I'm on study leave,' I said.

Charity made a noise that sounded like *hmmpf* and then went back to sorting through a stack of books.

I wandered about in general fiction for a bit and then I sat down on one of the soft chairs and flicked through some magazines. They were pretty boring though. There were history magazines and chat magazines and others about cars and furniture and foreign holidays — but not a single one about maths. So I sat and read all the problem pages in every single copy of *Bliss* that I could find, and then – as soon as one became spare – I took a seat in front of a computer. And once I'd logged on I did what everybody else does when they're sitting in that seat. I clicked the internet icon and typed *www.facebook.com* into the browser.

Perhaps it would have been better if I hadn't.

My homepage looked something like this:

facebook   Jody Barton

42 notifications   WHAT'S ON YOUR MIND?

17 friend requests

friends (311)   NATALIE SNELL
                    OMG! YOUR GAY!!

Jolene Barton   LATASHA JOY
                    I NEW IT!!

KENNY SIMONS   MISHA MONKEY BOGDANCHIKOV
                    WASSUP GAY BOY?

Hamish Hamster   LEWIS EDMUNDSON
                    LOOK AT ME FUNNY
                    AND U R DEAD.

Without breathing, I scrolled down the page. I had forty-two new wall-posts and they were all hideous. But at least Jolene hadn't posted any of them.

Slowly, I started to breathe again and clicked on the friend requests. Every one of them was from somebody I hardly knew.

It's amazing how popular you get when people want to write abuse on your wall.

I clicked IGNORE FRIEND REQUEST seventeen times and then I folded my arms, sat back and stared at the screen. And this time I wasn't looking at the words. I was looking at the numbers. Because numbers are massively important. They don't just tell us about maths-related stuff, they tell us about everything. Not only do they help us to manage money and tell the time and bake cakes and make music and understand art – they also allow us to make sense of every aspect of our entire lives. And what the numbers on the screen were telling me was this:

I had 311 virtual friends and no sign of a single real one.

I've always known I'm a bit of a loner. But it still came as a bit of a shock.

'Oh my God,' I said out loud. 'That is sooo bad.' And then I clicked the button that took me to my personal settings and just deleted my whole account.

After that, I didn't do anything. I couldn't. I was too numb to move. So I put my head in my hands, closed my eyes and tried to make some sort of sense of my life. But it was hard. Very hard. I think my mind had gone numb too.

Eventually, several googolplexes later, I heard someone say, 'You OK there, bruv?'

I looked up. It was Mookie the Media Guy. He was leaning across a trolley full of DVDs and looking at me with a face that looked genuinely full-on bothered. Mookie is another one of the librarians. He's in charge of all the music, films and games, so everyone calls him Mookie the Media Guy. Mookie is younger and cooler than the other librarians and he has neat little dreds and special-edition trainers. There are some people in life that you know are sound even before you've heard them speak. I thought Liam Mackie was one of them, but he wasn't. Mookie is though.

He asked me again, 'You OK there, bruv?'

'Hm,' I said. 'I was just thinking about stuff.'

Mookie shrugged his shoulders. 'Must be pretty strong stuff. It's making your eyes water.'

'Oh.' I quickly rubbed my eyes on the sleeve of my boring v-neck. 'I've got hayfever,' I added.

Mookie nodded. 'Yeah. February is a bad month for pollen.' And then he scratched his chin, nodded at his trolley and said, 'I don't suppose you could give me a hand putting some of these films back on the shelf, could you?'

And because I couldn't think of anything else to say, I said, 'OK.'

I followed him over to the media section. It's not a part of the library I tend to use that much because you have to pay to borrow stuff.

Mookie said, 'You're doing me a big favour, bruv. These

films need to go back on the racks in alphabetical order. And anything that ain't in English needs to go in the World section. And anything that's a drama off the telly needs to go in the TV Drama section. And anyone that's having a laugh goes in the Stand-up Comedy section.' And then he plucked a copy of Justin Bieber's DVD, *Never Say Never*, from off the top shelf of his trolley and said, 'And that includes this little guy. Know what I'm saying, bruv?'

And I grinned then and said, 'Yeah,' because I totally did.

It took me over an hour to sort that trolley out. I reckon there were more than three hundred films on that trolley. Once I got started, Mookie wandered off to do something else and left me to get on with it. I didn't mind though. It was good to have something to do. It was good to take a break from thinking about myself and my life and who I was and why I'd kissed kissed Liam Mackie and why I didn't seem to have that many friends.

Mookie came back just as I was putting the last few films in their alphabetical homes. When he spotted the almost empty trolley, he smiled and said, 'Nice work, bruv.' And then he said, 'How's your hayfever?'

I frowned. And then I remembered my lie and said, 'It's a lot better, thanks. I feel a whole heap better.'

Mookie grinned. 'You know what, bruv. That's the healing power of film, that is.'

I frowned again. 'Is it?'

Mookie stopped grinning and nodded earnestly. 'Totally, bruv. Film is art, innit. And art is good for the soul.' And then he put his hand on my shoulder, steered me over to the shelves reserved for films beginning with D and said, 'Let me show you something.'

I let him. I didn't have anything else I needed to be doing.

Mookie waggled his finger along the racks and then said, 'Gotcha,' and pulled one of the empty DVD cases from the display rack.

It was for a film called *Do the Right Thing*. I'd never heard of it.

'This film' said Mookie, 'is culturally significant. It's not just entertainment – it's art. And it's the ninety-sixth best film ever made.' And then he waved his hand at all the racks and said, 'And there've been a lot of films made. What we've got here doesn't even scratch the surface.'

'I've never heard of it,' I said.

Mookie rolled his eyes. 'It's Spike Lee innit. From 1989. He wrote it, he directed it and he stars in it. What can I say? The man's a genius. I've lost count of how many times I've watched this film, but every time I see it I get something new out of it. And for one hundred and twenty minutes, I'm so busy soaking up the stuff on the screen that I stop worrying about life's little niggles. I don't even worry about the big niggles. And that, bruv, is the healing power of film.'

'Oh,' I said, and I put my hand out to take the DVD from him.

Mookie pulled his arm back so that the film case was just out of my reach. 'Whoa! Not yet. Not for you. It's a Certificate 18, innit. The language is a bit lively and a few bad things happen. As a responsible adult and an employee of Brent Council, I can't allow you to borrow this film. But you must have a favourite film that you love? One that totally ticks all your boxes?'

And I did. Of course I did. I just wasn't sure if it was the sort of film a guy my age ought to be massively into.

Mookie said, 'So come on then. What is it?'

I bit my lip and thought about saying something else. Something a bit more straightforward. Like . . .

ROCKY

or STAR WARS

or DIE HARD

or anything involving James Bond

or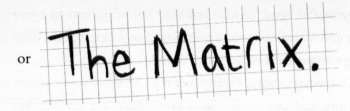

But then I just looked down at my hi-tops and said, 'It's an old film. You probably won't have even heard of it.'

'Try me,' said Mookie. 'I'm the Media Guy.'

So I took a deep breath and said, '*Running on Empty.*'

Mookie's face lit up. 'Directed by Sidney Lumet. 1988.' And then he nodded and said, 'It's a seriously good film.'

My face lit up too. 'You think so?'

'I *know* so,' said Mookie. 'It's about false identity and running away from reality until, finally, the central character, Danny Pope – played by River Phoenix – is forced to take a stand for who he really is and what he believes in. That ain't no stupid film. You can learn a lot from a film like that.'

And because I couldn't think of anything better to say, I asked again, 'Do you think so?'

And Mookie winked and said, 'I know so. So go home and watch it.'

So that's what I did.

I waited until half past three when I knew school would be finished and then I went home, dug out my copy of *Running on Empty* and popped it into the DVD player.

Mookie's right. It is a good film. A seriously good film. I always knew that – right from the very first time that I ever sat down and watched it. And it may not be tough like

Rocky or *Die Hard*, or futuristic and full of gadgets like *Star Wars* and *The Matrix* and *James Bond* but *I* like it and I'd be lying to myself if I pretended I didn't.

And, what's more, I'd be lying if I said that I could watch that film and not think about how much my heart aches whenever I look at River Phoenix.

Because it does. It absolutely does.

And to pretend it doesn't is to run away from who I really am. And why should I do that? I deserve my own chance.

THE G-WORD

The next morning, I didn't even bother with my school uniform. Or the sensible v-neck. I just put on some proper clothes and stomped out of the house before anyone had a chance to speak to me. And then I zipped up my coat, pulled down my hat and walked the mile and a bit to Kilburn High Road.

Normally I don't like walking. I'd rather get on the bus or the tube or borrow a bike or do anything other than walk. But this time I didn't mind. And I didn't even mind that it was dark and drizzly and probably cold enough to do my acorns some serious damage. Because I had a plan. And, even though it wasn't much of a plan, it was firing up my insides a whole lot more than when I had no plan at all.

It was this:

1. Go to Kilburn Market and reclaim my sense of self.
2. Go home and tell my mum everything.

It's what you call a systematic approach to problem solving. Mrs Hamood, my maths teacher, reckons that when you have a complicated problem, it's better to employ a systematic approach and break it into small logical steps rather than attempt to solve the whole thing at once. Which is fine with maths problems, but much trickier with real-life ones. Because sometimes in life there *aren't* any small steps.

Only very big ones.

But, because I'd had enough of feeling like a spineless, lily-livered wimp, I tried not to think about Step Two and forced myself to stay focused on Step One. And this was a lot less scary because all it really involved was buying a couple of posters.

When I reached Kilburn High Road, the shops were still shut and the market traders were only just beginning to open up. Sandy's Snack Shack, Flossie's Flowers and Hairy Poppins (the unisex hairstylist) were already doing business, but most of the other stalls were still hidden behind metal shutters. I bought myself a cup of tea from Sandy and waited for the Poster Hut to open. And while I stood there, sheltering under Sandy's canvas roof and sipping my hot tea, I watched Kilburn come to life.

There was a lot to look at.

I saw council workers sucking up the rubbish with rubbish-sucking machines and a fat man in a van delivering crates of bananas and a woman using the wing mirror of the fat man's van to do her eye make-up and three blokes in Argos uniforms yawning as they waited for Argos to open and an old lady – who was also waiting for Argos to open – shuffling around in a pair of gold trainers and a Chinese man cleaning the window of the Hard Wok cafe and a young guy with huge headphones walking three tiny white dogs and two little kids in dark green blazers holding the hands of a young woman in a nanny's uniform and bigger kids in cheap puffa jackets holding bacon rolls and girls who looked hardly any older than me pushing babies in scruffy buggies and women in suits blowing the steam off their coffees and a guy with a balaclava-beard picking stuff out of a litter bin and a man in a Beamer shouting at a traffic warden and businessmen barking into phones and barrow boys shouting and pensioners chatting and posers posing and hipsters being cool and hangarounds hanging around and you name it . . . I blinking well saw it.

And I suppose that's what I love about London. All human life is here. There are 7,172,091 people in this city and they come in every shape and size and colour and personal specification that you could possibly ever imagine.

And when you put yourself into that context it's pretty hard to feel strange even if you actually want to.

'Hello, sweetheart. Waiting for me?'

I looked up and smiled. It was the nice woman who runs The Poster Hut. I'd recognize her anywhere because she's got blue hair and a tattoo of a seahorse on her neck.

'You wouldn't give me a hand opening up, would you, lovely?'

I smiled again and nodded and helped her push up the metal shutters of the stall.

'Thanks,' she said. 'Tell you what. If there's anything you want from the Sale rack, I'll let you have it for free.'

'Ta,' I said, and glanced over to where she was indicating. I could see a massive picture of the kid from the *Home Alone* films and another one of Peter Andre. They weren't even worth having for free. 'Actually,' I said, 'I know what I'm after. Have you got any River Phoenix posters?'

The woman frowned and stroked her seahorse. 'Think so. Usually keep River in stock. Most kids these days have never heard of him, but the ones who have absolutely love him.'

'Do they?' I pushed back my beanie hat and looked at her hopefully. 'Even guys?'

Poster Woman frowned again and began to flick through a rack of film stars. 'Well, now you mention it, I suppose it *is* mostly the girls who want a picture of River. But some lads do as well. And why not? We're not all pressed from the same pastry cutter, are we?'

'Nope,' I said. Because she's right.

'Here we go,' she said. 'I think this is the only one I've got at the moment.'

I looked. It was the picture of River wearing the red jacket and red trousers and the great big pair of boots. I've always thought he looks really lovely in that shot. But so lonely too. Although he isn't *really* alone, is he? It's just a question of perspective. There are 7,172,091 people just in London and when you take into account all the others who live in Paris and New York and Hong Kong and Moscow and Mexico City and every single other place on the map, that's a seriously large number of people. So the chances are that everybody has at least one friend waiting in the wings to keep them company. And in this poster it's the cameraman who is standing right in front of River's face.

'Yeah, that'll do,' I said. 'I need another as well. Have you got any pictures of The Doors?'

Poster Woman smiled. 'I've always got loads.' She waved her hand at the racks containing rock bands and said, 'Have a shufty through those. There should be several of Jim Morrison and his mates amongst that lot.'

And there were. I actually had a choice of twelve different posters. Jim looked cool in all of them but, in the end, I decided not to mess around and chose a big one which was *just* of him and not the others. It seemed more honest. Jim has always been my favourite member of The Doors. He's the reason I buy the posters. There's no way I'd have pictures of Ray Manzarek and Robby Krieger and John Densmore on my wall otherwise.

Poster Woman rolled up my purchases tightly and put them into a cardboard tube to protect them from the rain. 'Treating yourself today or someone else?'

'These are mine,' I said, and handed over my money. And then I started smiling again. But this time my smile wasn't directed at the woman – it wasn't directed at anyone. It was just one of those unstoppable expressions of happiness you get when things are feeling good. And for the first time in ages they finally were feeling good. Because it was such a massive relief to know that my bedroom would soon be back to normal again.

When I got home, my mum and dad were both busy in the cafe. As soon as my mum saw me, she stopped wiping tables and said, 'Why were you in such a rush to get out this morning? I bet you didn't even have any breakfast, did you?' And straight after that she said, 'Why aren't you at school?'

I shot a quick glance at my dad. He was emptying the fridge of unsold cartons of orange drink and hadn't even noticed me. In a low voice, I said, 'I need to talk to you.'

'You need to be in school, that's what you need to be doing,' said my mum.

'Mum,' I said – very calmly – 'I really do need to talk to you.' And then I remembered my manners and added, 'Please.'

My mum gave me a funny look which was half-smile and half-frown. Then she wiped her hands on her apron and said, 'You go on upstairs. I'll be with you in about ten minutes. I just need to help your dad get the macaroni cheese sorted out. We can't have the customers going hungry, can we?'

'Thanks,' I said. 'I'll be in my room.'

I hurried through the STAFF ONLY door and ran up the stairs to my bedroom at the top of the building. Then, as soon as I was safely inside, I flumped down on my bed and did some very controlled b-r-e-a-t-h-i-n-g. I had too. I'd have suffocated otherwise. All of a sudden, I was so short of breath that I sounded like a swimmer with a dodgy snorkel. It surprised me. I run up and down those stairs all the time and I'm not usually so unfit. But, then again, I'm not usually on the verge of telling everything to my mum either. That kind of conversation could steal anyone's oxygen.

When I'd stopped suffocating, I stood up and walked up and down the length of my room a few times. It only took three paces. I sat down on my bed again. And then I remembered my posters, found some Blu-Tack and stuck them on the wall. Immediately, I felt better. It was good to see River and Jim again. It was like having a couple of old friends back. Except that they were the kind of friends you secretly have a massive crush on.

I stood up and started pacing around again and, as I paced, my mind kept turning over a single question. It was a very different question to any previous ones. It was this:

How long does it take to make macaroni cheese?

Because I knew that as soon as that macaroni cheese was made, my life was never ever going to be quite the same again.

I put my thumbnail in my mouth and bit it. And then I remembered something. Lifting up an edge of my mattress, I slid my hand underneath it and pulled out an ex-crumpled, bed-flattened booklet. It was the one that Superman had given me.

Am I gay/lesbian/bisexual?

'Shit,' I said, for no particular reason. And then I opened it up and started to read.

> Did you know that an estimated one in every ten people is gay/lesbian/ bisexual?

No, I didn't know that.

> That's about the same proportion of the population as people who have blonde hair.

Can't be right, I thought. I know shed-loads of people with blonde hair but I'm the only boy in my school who fancies other boys.

> So being gay is just as natural and ordinary as being straight.

Try telling Liam Mackie that. Or my dad.

> So how do you know if you're gay/ lesbian/bisexual?

Well, I know for definite that I'm not a lesbian, thank you very much.

> It's sometimes difficult to answer this question when you're a teenager because life is so interesting and exciting that your emotions are shifting around all the time. Enjoy exploring who you are.

Jog. Right. Off.

> But often you'll know that how you feel is *not* just a passing phase. Make a

list of all the people you've ever been attracted to. Are they males or females or both?

I've only ever fancied Liam Mackie, I thought. And then I bit my thumbnail and frowned because I knew that was actually only half of the truth. The other half is that I've never fancied girls. Not ever. Not Natalie Snell. Not Latasha Joy with her big gazongas. Not Beyoncé Knowles. Not Cheryl Cole. Not even Pippa Middleton. I like some girls and I think some girls are really pretty but I haven't ever wanted to kiss one. And I've always felt completely different because of that.

And who are the pin-ups covering your walls? It may seem silly, but it's the little details like these which may be clues to who you really are.

'River Phoenix,' I said out loud. And then – just in my head – I added, 'He's so bloody beautiful!'

A lot of people ask themselves, 'Why am I gay?'

Yep. Fair point.

It's just who you are. Nothing has made you gay/lesbian/bisexual. Would you be asking yourself the question, 'Why am I straight?'

Nope.

So don't then! Don't feel embarrassed. Respect yourself and the way you are. ☺

There was a whole load more of this stuff, but I didn't read it because I could hear footsteps coming up the stairs. Quickly, I shoved the leaflet back under my bed and then for no reason that I can properly explain, I rushed over to my window and checked that the arch of Wembley Stadium was still smiling in the sky over north-west London.

It was.

I breathed out a big sigh of relief and crossed my fingers.

My mum poked her head round the edge of my door and said, 'Can I come in then?'

I nodded and sat back down on my bed.

My mum stepped into my room, pulled the chair out from under my desk and sat down. She looked nervous.

'What's going on, Jody? Why aren't you at school? I think I put too much pepper in the macaroni cheese because I couldn't concentrate – I've been worrying so much.'

I bit my knuckle and thought about the bombshell I was about to drop. And then I said, 'Sorry.'

My mum waved my apology away. 'Oh, don't worry about it. It's only macaroni cheese.'

'Nah,' I said. 'It's not that. I mean . . . I'm not really bothered about the macaroni cheese. Well, I am . . . but that's not really what I'm apologizing for. It's a kinda much wider issue than macaroni cheese, to be honest.'

My mum leaned forward and put her hand on my arm. 'Just tell me.'

'I'M GAY,' I said. And then I clapped my hand over

my mouth. I hadn't meant to tell her quite so loudly.

My mum's eyebrows rose by about two centimetres. Her hand stayed on my arm though.

After a few seconds, she said, 'Are you sure?'

'OF COURSE I'M SURE,' I snapped. And then I clapped my hand back over my mouth again because snapping at people doesn't ever really help much.

My mum said, 'OK, OK. I was just asking. I don't know much about these things, Jody.'

'Neither do I,' I said more quietly. 'I just know that I *am*.'

My mum got off the chair and came and sat down next to me on the bed.

'And this is why you're not at school today?'

'Yep,' I said. 'I can't face it at the moment.' And then I hesitated before adding, 'I haven't been to school all week.'

My mum's eyes widened. And then she looked annoyed and said, 'I blame that school. They should've phoned me.'

I shrugged. 'You should blame me. I'm the one who hasn't been in.'

My mum sighed and then nodded and looked thoughtful. 'Has that black eye got anything to do with this?'

'Yep,' I said. And then I looked down at my hi-tops and said, 'Liam hit me because he knew I fancied him.'

My mum's eyes widened a bit more and then she sighed again and said, 'Blimey, Jody, you could have picked someone who wasn't going out with your sister. Talk about making life hard for yourself.'

'I didn't *choose* to fall in love with him,' I said.

My mum's eyebrows shot up again. 'You fell in love with him?'

I shrugged and put my head in my hands. 'I thought I did. It felt like it at the time.' And then I closed my mouth and stopped talking because I could feel myself getting upset.

My mum went quiet for quite a long time. I sat on my bed – head in hands – and waited for her to get upset as well.

But she didn't.

Instead, she wrapped her arms around me, pulled me towards her and just said, 'Oh, Jody!'

I was so surprised that I let myself be hugged for a few seconds and then I pulled away and said, 'You seriously don't mind?'

My mum smiled. 'It's a bit of a shock. But why should I mind? I just want you to be happy, Jode.'

'Oh,' I said. I couldn't think of a single other thing to say. To be honest, I'd expected the conversation to be more complicated.

'And besides,' said my mum with a smile, 'I always knew you were special.'

'Oh,' I said again. And then I frowned. What the hell was she talking about?

'But I'm not special,' I said. 'I'm gay but I'm not *special*. About one in ten people are thought to be gay, lesbian or bisexual. That's about the same proportion of the population as people who have blonde hair. I'm just ordinary.'

'Oh,' said my mum, and she frowned too. But then she brightened up again and said, 'But you've always been special to me, Jody, and you always will be. My little leap-day baby! You don't get born on the twenty-ninth of February just to follow the crowd.'

'Yeah,' I said, 'but that's not why I'm gay. It's got nothing to do with my birthday or my star sign or my past life or anything. It's just who I am.' I was starting to feel a bit agitated.

'I know,' said my mum. 'And it's exciting really, isn't it?'

'*Is* it?' I was getting more agitated by the second.

'Yeah,' said my mum. 'It's just like having our very own Rufus Wainwright in the family.'

I stared at her, totally baffled. And then I said, 'Who the heck is Rufus Wainwright?'

My mum said, 'Oh, surely you've heard of him! He's that American singer-songwriter. Or is he Canadian? Camp as Christmas. Gorgeous-looking though.' And then she scrunched up her forehead to think about it a bit harder and said, 'He's sort of like a gay James Blunt.'

My mouth dropped open in alarm. 'Oh my God!'

My mum giggled. 'Oh, chill out a bit, Jody. It's no big deal.' And then she looked serious again and said, 'Does Jolene know?'

'Yeah,' I said, and bit my lip.

My mum squeezed my arm. 'She'll get used to the idea, sweetheart. You did try to hit on her boyfriend so don't be too down on her.'

'I'm not down on her,' I said. 'She's down on me.'

My mum said, 'Who else knows?'

'Everybody at school. They've been talking about me on Facebook.'

My mum sighed and squeezed my arm again. 'You can't stay off school forever though, can you? You've got to face up to things. You've got your GCSEs in a few months.'

'I know,' I said. 'But there's only tomorrow and then it's half-term. And after that I'll be ready to deal with it. Don't make me go back tomorrow.'

My mum fiddled with her hair. 'But you can't mope around here all day. What will we say to your dad?'

'We'll tell him the truth,' I said. 'You just said I've got to face up to things.'

My mum fiddled with her hair a bit harder. 'Yeah, but, sweetheart, there's no point rushing into anything. Just give it a few days until you're sure. And, if you really are, tell your dad *then*.'

'But I'm sure now,' I said.

This time it was my mum who bit her lip. 'I know you are, darling. But I don't know how well your dad is going to deal with the G word. When it comes down to it, he's a very traditional man with very traditional ideas. He absolutely hated that film *Brokeback Mountain*. So let's not worry him with this for the time being.'

ON GLADSTONE HILL

I'm not sure whether I felt better or worse after that. I definitely felt a bit flat though and also a little like I'd been cheated. It was as if I'd just dragged myself all the way up Mount Everest only to find that there was an even bigger mountain standing right behind it. And, worse than that, I'd been greeted at the top by a gay version of James Blunt who had high-fived me and told me that we were both as camp as Christmas and just like two gay peas in a glittery gay pod.

So as soon as my mum was out of my room I put on Call of Duty and spent the next few hours liberating France. And by the time I'd bored myself of that, I felt less like a gay pea and slightly more like Action Man.

But dinner that evening was as awkward as ever. Dodgy looks were being passed around our table more frequently than the salt and pepper pots. Every time I looked Jolene's way, I found myself on the receiving end of a Vulcan Death Glare. In the end I had to stop looking at her.

Then there was my mum. She was acting proper weird. For a start, she was fussing around me and being overly nice – which would have been OK if I hadn't spotted the funny glances she kept flashing me. Every few seconds, we'd catch each other's eye and I'd see a look of pure panic staring back at me. At first I couldn't work it out. And then it dawned on me that she actually thought I was going to stand up at any second and proclaim my gayness at the dinner table.

It put me off my macaroni cheese, if I'm honest.

The only person who was acting normally was my dad. He ate a few mouthfuls of macaroni and then waved his fork at me and Jolene and said, 'Are you two kids still having an epic communication fail?'

I can't cope when my dad tries to talk hip. It's embarrassing.

Jolene pulled a face and said, 'Nobody says epic communication fail, Dad. It's called an epic conversation fail. And, yes, we are.'

My dad said, 'Why? What's the beef?'

I cringed. I think Jolene did too. My mum sprang up from her seat and said, 'Does anyone want the ketchup?'

Jolene just said, 'Ask Jody.'

My dad looked at me and said, 'So what's the beef, sunshine?'

I pushed a piece of macaroni around with my fork and

didn't say anything. My dad stared at me for a moment and then rolled his eyes and said, 'Crikey O'Mighty! You two are as much fun as a day out in Watford! Whatever it is, just make sure you've smoothed it over before your birthday. I'm not having you turning sixteen – or four – and not being on friendly terms. So that gives you almost a fortnight to sort yourselves out.'

Jolene puckered up and made a farting noise. And then she said, 'Jog. Right. Off.'

Sometimes she's so rude that I struggle to accept we're twins.

My dad said, 'Watch your manners, Loopy Lou.' And then he turned to me and said, 'When are you gonna start helping me in the cafe again? You're not still feeling iffy, are you?'

I pushed my macaroni around a bit more.

My dad said, 'Those two old dears have been asking after you. What are their names again? Rita and Maureen? Yeah, they've missed you.'

'Have they?' I suddenly felt extremely anxious. I hoped they hadn't told my dad that they'd seen me sitting in Super Burger at Brent Cross.

'Yeah,' said my dad. 'They can't get enough of you . . . think you're the bee's knees. And Whispering Bob Harris . . . he's been asking after you as well.'

I raised my eyebrows. 'Has he?'

My dad turned ever so slightly red. Then he smiled and said, 'Well . . . no . . . I made that bit up, obviously. Whispering Bob Harris doesn't like anyone, does he?

And actually . . . those two old birds didn't ask about you either . . . but *I* miss having you around, Jode. Nobody else washes up quite as well as you.'

And even though Jolene was giving me the Vulcan Death Glare and my mum was flashing me looks of panic, I started to laugh a bit. I couldn't help it.

'OK Dad,' I said. 'Just shout whenever you want a hand.'

My dad beamed and said, 'Good lad. But stay safe, yeah? It's only a little over a week until we make our holy Hotspur pilgrimage to Wembley Stadium. Chunky and Son. I can't blinking wait.'

And Jolene made that horrible farty noise with her mouth again and my mum suddenly looked as if she was about to give birth to a kitten and, even though I quite like macaroni cheese, the moment that I was excused and able to escape back to my bedroom didn't come a single second too soon.

The next morning, my mum stuck her head round my door and said, 'You can't mope around here all day, Jody. I want you to get dressed and ready for school.'

'Oh, Muuuum,' I groaned, 'it's the last day before the half-term holiday. You said I could take today off.'

'No I didn't,' said my mum. 'You don't listen properly.'

'Well, I'm not going,' I said. 'I can't face it. Not yet.'

My mum looked agitated. 'You can't stay at home though. What will we tell your dad? That you've got a mouldy foot or something?'

I sighed heavily and pulled the duvet up over my head.

My mum said, 'It's just one day, Jode. One single day.'

223

I pulled the duvet back down, sat up and said, 'If you make me go to school today, I'll . . . I'll start smoking.'

Even as I was saying it, I knew it was a pretty lame bargaining tool. But at that exact second it was the most persuasive argument I could think of.

My mum blew out her cheeks and made that puh sound. Then she said, 'It'll make your clothes whiff and your hair pong and turn your teeth yellow, but . . . OK then.'

'Oh, Muuuuum,' I said. 'I really don't want to go.'

My mum chewed her lip for a moment. And then she said, 'Jody, just get ready for school, get through today and I'll see you back here at half-three.'

'I'm not going,' I said.

'I know, sweetheart. I *heard* you,' said my mum. 'But I don't think you're hearing me. So get up, get yourself out of the house and I'll see you later.' And then she made her eyes go all big and round as if she was trying to send me some sort of telepathic message and said, '*Hmmm?*'

'Ohhhh,' I said. 'You mean I don't have to—'

'And,' added my mum, 'if I hear after half-term that you've skipped another single day of school, I'll be walking you there myself.' And then she shoved a fiver into my hand, kissed me on the cheek and hurried off.

I don't know what my teachers think of my mum but I love her.

So I played along, put my school uniform on and left the house.

It was cold outside. It usually is in Willesden Green in

February. I walked around the block a couple of times and then I went to the library to see if Mookie was about. He wasn't. But Charity was. She looked at me from behind a pile of books and said, 'Shouldn't you be somewhere?'

'I'm on study leave,' I said.

Charity made a noise that sounded like *hmmpf*. Then she said, 'Still?'

'Yeah,' I said, 'still. Is Mookie around?'

'He's on a training day,' said Charity. 'He's learning stuff. Just like you do when you go to school. And if I phoned your school would they tell me you're on study leave?'

'Oh my days,' I said. 'What is this? Twenty questions? I only asked if Mookie was in.' And then I turned round and rushed straight out, leaving Charity shaking her head and *hmmpfing* behind me.

I didn't know what to do after that so I took another walk around the block. I was pretty cold and pretty fed up, to tell the truth. I was also pretty bored because I was seeing the exact same stuff that I saw the last time I did that circuit. Willesden Green doesn't change much in the space of ten minutes. I saw kebab shops and nail bars and buses and mini-cabs and tanning salons and tattoo parlours and hurrying people and hamburger wrappers and fly-posters and falafel bakers and all the usual stuff that I've seen a nonillion times before.

But then I stopped.

Because on a wall, close to where Willesden High

Road merges with Neasden Lane, I saw something new. Something so new that it hadn't even been there ten minutes earlier.

In big black letters, somebody had sprayed these words:

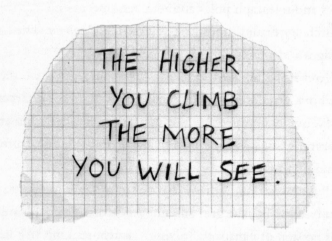

THE HIGHER
YOU CLIMB
THE MORE
YOU WILL SEE.

Fair enough, I thought. And taking it as some sort of sign I turned round and began to walk in the direction of the closest high place that I know. The hill on Gladstone Park.

Sixteen minutes later, I was huffing and puffing and leaning forward against the railing of the duck pond at the very top of the hill. On the other side, most of the ducks had disappeared and the ones that were still around had their heads folded away under their wings.

'That's nice,' I said to them. 'I've walked all the way up this hill to see you and you can't even be bothered to show your little ducky faces.'

So I gave up on them and turned round to take in the view over north London. And, even though I'd seen it a

decillion times before, it still managed to completely blow my breath away.

Beyond the park, just about as far as the eye could see, was a crazy sprawl of high-rise flats and flyovers and train lines and telegraph poles and minarets and phone masts and church spires and superstores and office blocks and railway bridges and warehouses and rooftops.

And rising up above the whole lot, like a massive metal rainbow, was the enormous white arch of Wembley Stadium.

'Wow,' I whispered – because although it probably isn't everybody's idea of a beautiful view it really did look pretty stunning to me.

I followed the path of the giant arch with my eye. It disappeared into the grey silhouette of north London. There was no sign of a giant pot of gold anywhere.

And then I stopped staring into the far distance and looked at the scene unfolding much closer to me.

On the other side of the park, a group of boys were running into view. They looked wet and a bit muddy and were all dressed in matching gold rugby shirts and black shorts.

The PE kit of my school.

The school where everyone was talking about me and posting crappy messages on Facebook.

I immediately lost about one metre thirty in height and crouched down on the balls of my feet. It's an invisibility tactic I've picked up from Call of Duty.

At the front of the pack were all the Sport Boys – the

ones who play in the school teams and who always get picked first by the team captains. It was obvious they hadn't spotted me. They all had their heads tilted skyward and were cross-country running with a very definite and determined sense of purpose. I relaxed a bit but stayed where I was, low to the ground. Way down the hill, the Sport Boys ran by and headed off towards the park's south gate. I relaxed a bit more.

After the Sport Boys, came a long thin line of everybody else. Their heads weren't tilted skyward and they weren't running with the same obvious sense of focus. I noticed Besnik Bogdan from my chemistry class had his mobile phone pressed against his ear as he ran and a couple of other boys had stopped under a big tree to have a smoke. But none of this lot saw me either. I waited a while for them all to pass and then, when the coast was clear, I stood up again and stamped the numbness out of my aching feet.

But then one more runner came into view.

Although he was more of a *walker* than a runner. And a very slow walker at that. He was huffing and puffing and had his hand pressed into his side as if he was trying to deaden the pain of the world's most hideous cross-country-running stitch.

And the second I saw him everything changed. Because it suddenly dawned on me that those crappy Facebook messages didn't actually matter. The people who wrote them weren't proper friends anyway. They were virtual friends. Come to think of it, they weren't even that.

They were idiots.

And, even though there were 311 of them, they weren't worth half of the slow-moving stitch-inflicted guy in front of me.

Not caring whether any of the other runners heard me or not, I took a big deep breath and as loudly as I could I shouted, 'CHATTY!' And then I waved my arms above my head and began running down the hill towards him.

Chatty Chong looked my way and stopped. And then he saw me, frowned and started walking again.

'Chatty . . . wait,' I shouted.

Chatty walked as far as the big tree and then stopped and leaned against the trunk. I ran over to him, finally slowing to a stop as I approached. My hand was pressed hard against a pain in my side. Somehow, even in that short distance, I'd developed a stitch.

We were both quiet for a moment while I got my breath back and then Chatty said, 'If you've come to tell me I'm a geek, don't bother. I don't need it, yeah? I already know.'

I looked down at my hi-tops. They'd got so muddy that I knew they'd never be quite as good ever again. Normally this would have upset me a bit, but, right then, it didn't really seem important.

'I'm sorry,' I said.

Chatty Chong looked down at the ground and kicked at a tuft of grass and then he tilted his head skyward, looked over towards Wembley and said, 'Yeah, well . . . you should be . . . so don't try saying it again, yeah?'

'I won't,' I said. 'I'm an idiot.'

Chatty frowned and seemed to think about this and then he nodded and said, 'Yeah.'

Even though it probably wasn't a smiling situation, I smiled anyway. I couldn't help it. Chatty Chong doesn't exactly say much, but you always know where you are with him.

He jerked his head at me and said, 'What happened to your eye?'

'I smashed it really hard against someone's fist,' I said.

Chatty's eyebrows rose and a look of shock flashed across his face. 'Ouch,' he said.

I nodded. 'Yeah. Ouch.'

Chatty said, 'I didn't see you in Maths Club. In fact, I ain't seen you in maths lessons either. You ain't been in all week, yeah?'

'I've had some stuff to sort out,' I said.

Chatty's eyebrows rose a bit more and his cheeks went red. And then he said, 'I heard that horrible girl with the great big airbags telling everyone that you're gay, yeah?'

I think my cheeks went a bit red too. I looked down at the ground and kicked at a tuft of grass and muttered, 'Yeah. I am.' There wasn't anything else to say really.

Chatty nodded and looked a bit worried. 'You still like maths though, yeah?'

I looked up at him in surprise. 'Of course I do. I'm still me.'

Chatty heaved out a sigh and looked relieved, 'No drama

then, yeah?' And then he looked a bit hopeful and said, 'Do you wanna come over to my house later? I've found this new maths game. It's crap but it's quite funny, yeah? It's called Harry Potter and the Discontinuous Function.'

And I laughed out loud and nodded and had this really sudden urge to shake Chatty Chong firmly by the hand.

I didn't though because that sort of thing looks fine if you're both wearing a suit, but really weird when either of you is wearing a PE kit. So instead, I said 'That sounds good, yeah,' and I finally felt my world shift back somewhere closer to normal.

It was half-term after that. Half-term holidays always whizz by far too quickly in my life. They're mostly filled up with doing these things:

- Lying in bed asleep
- Lying in bed listening to The Doors
- Lying in bed doing nothing
- Hanging around the Hollister shop
- Hanging around The Poster Hut
- Hanging around the library
- Generally hanging around
- Doing maths with Chatty Chong
- Doing GCSE coursework
- Generally doing nothing

- Watching telly
- Watching River Phoenix films
- Generally watching my back
- Playing games on my Xbox
- Playing Laser Tag in the Trocadero
- Generally playing it cool
- Helping my dad in the cafe

That stuff may not sound especially taxing, but I still never manage to get it all done.

But *this* half-term was different. I wasn't in the mood for any general hanging around. In fact, I was so stressed out by the prospect of telling my dad about The G Situation that I wasn't in the mood for much really. Not even Laser Tag. So the first few days of my holiday were pretty much spent doing this . . .

- Staying out of Jolene's way
- Working in the cafe
- Going around Chatty Chong's house to play Harry Potter and the Discontinuous Function

And aside from me and Chatty smashing each other's high scores, nothing very interesting happened. Vee and Doreen came in and discussed *Strictly Come Dancing*, Whispering Bob Harris fell asleep in his apple pie and my dad told me again and again how much he was looking forward to taking me to the League Cup final.

'Ain't long now, sunshine,' he said to me every single morning. '*This* Saturday! Can you flipping believe it?'

And every single morning, I just shrugged and said, 'Yeah. Why not?' Because Spurs reaching a final wasn't *such* a difficult thing to get my head around. I mean, it's not like being told that every circle's circumference is approximately 3.14159265358979323846 26433832795028841971 69399375108209749445923078164062862089986 862 8034825342117 0679821480865132823 times as long its diameter – but that the exact ratio isn't known because mathematicians have only been able to calculate this number up as far as the first one trillion decimal places.

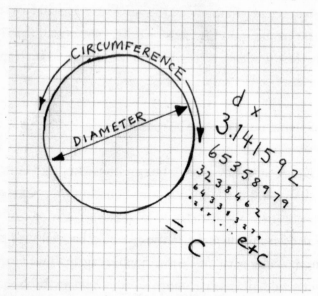

I find that kind of thing much more of a struggle to deal with than Spurs reaching a poxy cup final. Even though I love maths.

I also found it quite a struggle to stay out of Jolene's way. Seeing as how she was working in the cafe alongside me, this isn't all that surprising. Every time I stood at the counter, Jolene kept her distance on the cafe floor and every time I went and did anything on the cafe floor, Jolene went and stood by the counter. In the end, I made things simpler for both of us and claimed the territory around the sink as my base camp. This suited everyone. When it comes to washing up, nobody in our family does it even halfway as good as I do.

And then, on the Friday, Liam Mackie walked in.

For a moment, I just froze.

Since he punched me in the face, I'd had a lot of time to think about what I'd do if I saw him again. Twelve days, in fact.

That's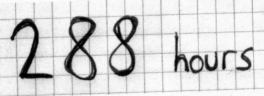

288 hours

235

or **17,280** minutes

or **1,036,800** seconds.

And I have to admit that a small proportion of that time had been spent picturing myself switching from NORMAL MODE to AIM DOWN THE SIGHT MODE and causing some serious grief to Liam Mackie's Damage Indicator.

But only a very small proportion.

Because mostly I tried to throw these thoughts out of my head. I like to think that I'm better than that. I like to think that I'm more like Mohandas Karamchand Gandhi and that I can win my battles peacefully and with my dignity intact.

But unfortunately when Liam walked in I had my jaws clamped around a fried-egg sandwich.

As soon as my momentary shock paralysis passed, I dropped the sandwich back down on to my plate, wiped my mouth with the back of my hand and frantically looked around for back-up. There wasn't any. Other than Whispering Bob Harris who was nodding off over a fish-finger baguette, the cafe was empty. My mum was across the road having a full Willesden Wonder Tan, Jolene was upstairs on a tea break and my dad was in his office pretending to do the accounts but actually playing Angry Birds.

I was on my own.

Liam sauntered over towards me, bold as brass. He still looked buff. He always will do, I suppose. He was wearing that moss-green parka again. It made him look as if he'd just escaped from Call of Duty. On a reflex, I tensed up and prepared myself for an enemy attack.

Liam leaned against the counter, tapped his own chin and said, 'You missed a bit . . . Jolene. That is your name, isn't it? Or Josephine or Joanne or Jomosexual or something?'

I stood up straighter and lifted my chin up and – very calmly – I said, 'Did you want something?'

Liam smirked. 'Not especially. But I was just passing by and I got this sudden urge for a smoothie. Is your mum in? I like her smoothies the best.' And then he grinned, leaned his elbows on the counter top and said, 'They're . . . well . . . tasty!'

And even though I knew that Mohandas Karamchand Gandhi definitely wouldn't approve, I curled my fist up into a ball and was a split second away from punching Liam right in the middle of his perfect face. I couldn't help it. He was making me so angry that my eyes had misted up.

But before I had a chance to even raise my fist, another voice rang out across the cafe and made me stop.

'My brother's name is *Jody*. And, NO, my mum *isn't* in, but my dad is and I think he'd like to have a word with you.'

Liam and I both turned to look at Jolene. She was standing by the STAFF ONLY door with her arms folded and an expression on her face that suggested she was as fed up as a sumo wrestler's flip-flop. For once, though, her strop seemed to be directed at Liam and not at me. She stood there for a second – just Vulcan Death Glaring – and then twisted her head and shouted, 'Dad, can you come out here a second.'

Liam's smirk disappeared and the colour drained from his face. I think it did from mine too. I knew that telling my dad I was gay was going to be hard *however* I approached it. But I still didn't want him to find out like *this*.

Liam took a few steps towards the cafe door. But then my dad appeared. He was smiling. As soon as he saw Liam, he stopped smiling and said, 'You've got a nerve, ain't you?'

Liam shrugged, flicked the hair out of his eyes with a sudden sideways jerk of the head and said, 'It's a free country.'

'Not to go around hitting people it ain't,' said my dad.

Liam shrugged again. 'So I hit him,' he said, and jerked his head at me. 'But only because I don't like being hit on. Know what I mean?'

I felt sick.

My dad looked confused.

Jolene said, 'Oh, grow up, Liam.' She said it quite loud. She must have done because it was enough to wake up Whispering Bob Harris, who jumped in his seat and bellowed, 'SPEAK UP, SON. I CAN'T HEAR YOU!'

My dad said, 'Kids, kids, let's keep it civil! I don't

wanna go upsetting our friendly cafe atmosphere.'

He looked at Liam and said, 'I'm sorry, son, I can't serve you. And I'd be very much obliged if you'd take your custom elsewhere in future.'

Liam said, 'But—'

And my dad said, 'But, as a parting gift, have one of these.' He reached behind the counter where a box of unsold cartons of orange juice was gathering dust, plucked out a single carton and pushed it into Liam's hands. 'There you go, boy. On the house. They're naturally and artificially flavoured, apparently. And made from concentrate.' My dad shook his head and sighed. 'I bought four hundred of those, but I just can't shift them. They look good – got lovely flashy packaging – but it turns out that they're rubbish through and through.' He gave Liam a meaningful nod and added, 'Know what I mean, Liam?'

Liam Mackie went red, tossed the carton of crap orange juice back at my dad and walked out. I haven't seen him since.

My dad stood there for a second looking very thoughtful and then he shook his head and said, 'QPR supporters. They're getting worse!' And with that he turned and disappeared back into his office.

Jolene and I stood there in silence for a moment. I don't know what she was thinking, but I know I was still stuck on that second where Liam had told my dad I'd hit on him. And all I could think about was whether or not my dad had heard and, if he *had* heard, whether he'd understood.

But then I pushed those thoughts aside because that was all stuff I could deal with when the time was right. At that precise second, I had a more immediate situation to handle.

'I know I've said this before,' I said, 'but I'm so very massively sorry, Jolene.'

Jolene looked down at her hi-tops. 'You should be,' she said.

'I am.'

Jolene nodded slowly. 'That stuff I said about finding a new twin – I didn't mean it.'

'Thanks,' I said. My eyes were prickling.

Jolene nodded again. 'And then she pushed her fringe out of her face and said, 'I'm still upset with you though.'

And *I* nodded slowly and said, 'That's fair enough.' I bit my thumbnail and said, 'Are you going to be upset with me forever?'

Jolene puffed out her cheeks until they made that puh sound. I carried on chewing my thumbnail and waited.

Finally, my sister shook her head and said, 'Nah. Only until you're sixteen. Or four.' And then she gave me a sweet little smile and I gave her one great big look of pure relief straight back.

And that pretty much ends the story of the biggest nuclear fallout me and my twin have ever had. Except for one final random detail. The moment after me and Jolene made our peace, Whispering Bob Harris pushed his chair back, stood up and said, 'Thank God for that.'

Surprised, we both turned to look at him. He pulled his

coat on, picked up his stick and said, 'All that drama ain't good for my digestion. You two have been giving me bad guts for days. And that Liam feller weren't worth tuppence anyway.'

Both mine and Jolene's jaws dropped open. But it was Jolene who managed to speak first. 'I thought you couldn't hear anything?'

Whispering Bob Harris frowned. 'What's that? Speak up, son. I can't hear you.'

'I thought you couldn't hear anything,' bellowed Jolene.

Whispering Bob Harris shrugged. 'My hearing ain't what it should be, right enough. But I can lip read. And, even though I'm old, I ain't daft, am I?'

He took a shuffling step or two towards the door, leaving Jolene and I standing side by side in gobsmacked silence. But then he stopped, turned and said, 'My name's Henry, by the way. How do you do?'

And, just like two peas in a pod, Jolene and I said, 'How do you do, Henry,' and we waved as he walked through the front door to take his place in the never-ending parade of interesting people who wander up and down Willesden High Road.

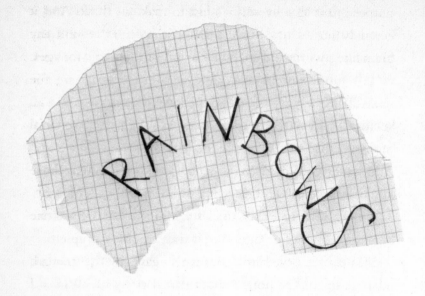

One thing I've learned is that life doesn't always follow a pretty pattern. Some days fall perfectly into place and quickly blend in with all the rest while other days are as random and as weird as the stuff Mrs Hamood tells us about in Maths Club.

Like the fact that four is the only number in the English language which is spelt using the right amount of letters.

Or that 111111111 x 111111111 = 12345678987654321.

Or that each person in the world shares their birthday with more than nineteen million other people. (Unless you happen to be a leapling like me – in which case you only share it with four million, seven hundred and ninety-one thousand, two hundred and thirty-nine others.)

And although this sort of stuff may sound utterly pointless I'm convinced it isn't. There *has* to be some mysterious purpose to it all – even if it's just to make us think. And it certainly makes me think because it wriggles around my brain like a worm and keeps me wondering about it for ages.

In a funny sort of way, life's random curveballs are the same. They may well feel like the kind of days we could all seriously do without, but they actually give us the crucial moments that make us stop and think about who we are. And while loads of easier days get quickly forgotten, those random curveballs end up living in our memories forever.

Falling head over heels in love with Liam Mackie was the biggest shocker of my life. And it was stressful and upsetting and it made my eye throb. But it also gave me the strength to speak up and be honest about who I really am. Which I always knew I *would* do just as soon as the time was right. It was simply a matter of deciding when that time was.

But in the end the moment chose itself. Me and my dad were sitting on a tube train and hurtling along the Jubilee Line towards Wembley. We weren't the only ones. The whole of north London was on that same train and almost everyone was wearing their tribal colours. White for Spurs. Red for Arsenal. There was also a serious amount of police in fluorescent yellow high-visibility jackets as well.

My dad leaned towards me and said, 'I can't believe we made it, sunshine. A League Cup final! And against Arsenal! What d'you reckon the score will be?'

My dad doesn't like Arsenal. He likes them even less than QPR.

I turned the question over in my mind for a second. I

didn't have a clue what the score would be. Or who might kick the ball into the net. Or even how the offside rule worked. The truth is that I've never been remotely fussed on football. But I didn't want to feel like an alien so I said, 'Five—nil to Spurs.'

But my dad didn't get the chance to hear my reply because at that exact same moment half the passengers in the carriage – the red half – started chanting, 'WE'LL WIN COS WE'RE AR-SE-NAL . . . WE'LL WIN COS WE'RE AR-SE-NAL . . . LA LA LA LA . . . LA LA LA LA.'

My dad looked outraged and did a big comedy roll of his eyes. And then he stood up from his seat, slapped his hands against his belly like he was banging some sort of chubby war drum and started chanting, 'WE LOVE YOU, TOTTENHAM, WE DO . . .'

The white half of the train broke out into cheers and began to chant along with him.

'WE LOVE YOU, TOTTENHAM, WE DO . . .'

I felt my face turn scaly and green, and alien antennae started sprouting out of my head – but I still laughed. I couldn't help it. My dad has that effect on me sometimes. To be fair, the fact that he was wearing a replica Spurs shirt with real cowboy spurs on his boots and a big white Stetson wasn't making it any easier to take him seriously.

My dad grinned down at me and paused from his chanting just long enough to shout, 'Come on, sunshine – give me a hand.'

And knowing that I had an entire afternoon of this kind of thing ahead of me I opened my mouth and added my voice to everyone else's.

'WE LOVE YOU, TOTTENHAM, WE DO . . . OHHHH, TOTTENHAM, WE LOVE YOU!'

And, even though I couldn't actually care less about the game, I have to admit that it was massively exciting to be part of the crowd and to be rushing towards Wembley on a wave of red and white and to be shouting and singing and stamping my feet to the only words we all seemed able to agree on.

'THERE'S ONLY ONE TEAM IN LONDON . . . ONE TEAM IN LOOOOO ONDON . . .'

By the time we all spilt off at Wembley Park, I was so buzzed up that my head was spinning off my shoulders. The sudden drop in temperature quickly made it slot back into place though. I pulled my sister's borrowed Spurs scarf up around my nose and followed my dad out of the tube station and down Olympic Way towards the stadium.

'Filthy weather for it,' said my dad as we walked head first into a wall of drizzle. 'Oh well, that's what happens when they insist on playing the final in February.'

I pulled my sister's borrowed Spurs hat down over my ears and hurried along next to him. If anything, the road to Wembley was even more packed than the tube train. There were Spurs fans and Arsenal fans and stewards and police and ticket touts and programme sellers and general wheeler-dealers and what looked to me pretty much like the entire match crowd of ninety thousand people all moving slowly together towards the giant white arch. I stayed close to my dad so that we wouldn't get separated.

And then, above all those ninety thousand different voices, I heard a girl's voice shout, 'OH MY DAYS, IS THAT JOLENE'S GAY BROTHER?'

And to my complete disbelief and horror another girl's voice shouted, 'YEAH, IT IS. I RECKON HE'S ONLY COME TO GET A LOOK AT SOME FIT LEGS.'

I stopped walking and looked up. Natalie Snell and Latasha Joy were grinning and waving at me. They were weaving their way through the crowd and carrying an armful of foam pointy hands printed with the Arsenal and Spurs logos.

Ninety thousand people, and I had to bump into *them*! I should start playing the lottery or something.

My dad stopped too and frowned. And then he said,

'D'you want a foam pointy hand?'

'No,' I said quickly. Because why the heck would I?

My dad nodded slowly. He was still frowning. 'Waste of money. We'll get a programme instead. Come on.'

He put his hand on my shoulder and we walked forward like that together – him steering me through the crowd. To be honest, it probably should have been *me* doing the steering because I'm at least half a head taller than he is – but I just went with it and put my legs on autopilot. Those stupid mouthy girls had upset me so much that my brain had shut down.

In front of us, a sea of red and white beanie hats bobbed closer and closer towards the big famous arch.

My dad squeezed my shoulder, put his voice close to my ear and said, 'Any thoughts about what you want for your birthday?'

'Not really,' I said.

My dad said, 'Well, start having a think.' And then he said, 'And what about Jolene?'

'I don't know what she wants,' I said.

'I didn't mean that,' said my dad. 'I meant have you two sorted out this monkey business that's been upsetting the pair of you?'

'I think so,' I said.

'Good,' said my dad, and patted my shoulder.

We walked on. Wembley Stadium loomed bigger and bigger in front of us. To see the arch, I now had to tilt my head skyward – just like those Sports Boys do when they're cross-country running.

My dad said, 'Is everything else OK?'

I stopped looking up at the arch and looked at my dad. And then my blood ran cold. Because, even though we were walking towards Wembley and he was about to see his beloved Tottenham Hotspur, he had a look of absolute agony on his face. I quickly looked down at my hi-tops and mumbled, 'I think so.'

My dad stopped walking. I did too. Around us, the red and white beanies continued to float past, slightly changing course as if we were some sort of awkward unexpected island. And then my dad put both his hands on both my shoulders, looked me right in the eyes and said, 'Are you sure there isn't anything you want to tell me, son?'

'I don't think so,' I said.

My dad lowered his arms, shoved his hands into his pockets and frowned down at his cowboy boots. For one terrible second, I actually thought he'd started to cry, but then I realized it was just the drizzle making his face wet.

The crowd continued to push past us.

My dad lifted his face again and said, 'You and me, boy – we're Chunky and Son. Don't ever forget that. But sometimes I worry that we don't speak the same lingo. Sometimes, I worry that we ain't even in the same solar system.'

And I don't know whether it was just the stupid drizzle or whether I'd started to cry without realizing it, but suddenly my face felt uncomfortably wet and I had to clench my jaw really hard to stop myself from bawling like a baby.

Tilting my head skyward, I looked up into the grey clouds and rested my eyes on the Wembley arch. And then

I looked back at my dad and just came straight out with it.

'I'm gay, Dad.'

For a moment, neither of us moved a muscle. We just stood there, the only stationary people in the middle of ninety thousand walking ones.

And then my dad said, 'Crikey O'Mighty! We don't half pick our moments.'

His eyes flicked away from mine. Something behind me had caught his attention.

I turned. High above the rooftops of Wembley, the sun had finally forced its way through the clouds. Where just a moment earlier I'd seen only varying shades of grey, a faint but fantastic rainbow was now shooting across the sky.

My dad said, 'Just tell me one thing, boy. You're not still holding a torch for that Liam muppet, are you?'

My jaw dropped in surprise.

My dad sighed. 'I might be getting old, son, but I'm not daft. Even a great big bonehead like me twigged in the end.'

I shook my head. 'You're not a bonehead.' And then I said, 'Do I like Liam? Definitely not!'

My dad nodded, satisfied. 'Thank God for that.' And then he put his guiding hand back on my shoulder and we both walked on towards the two great big rainbows in the sky.

And it was true what I told him. I don't fancy Liam Mackie any more. I don't even like him. But, even so, I won't ever forget him. Because he was the spark which lit the fire that changed my life.

And I'm totally cool with that.

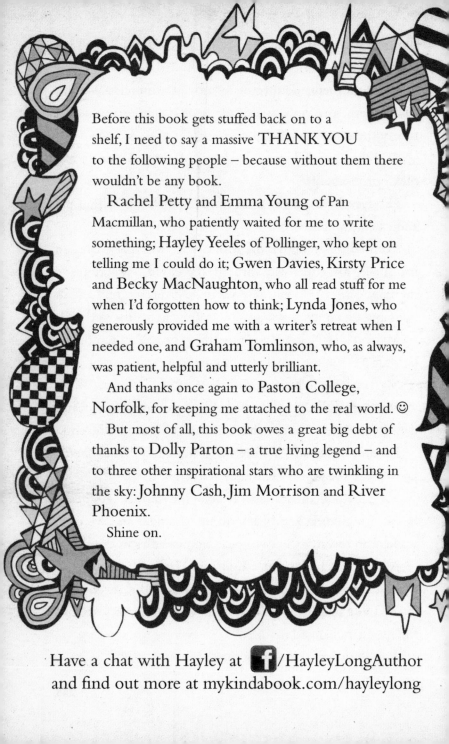

Before this book gets stuffed back on to a shelf, I need to say a massive THANK YOU to the following people – because without them there wouldn't be any book.

Rachel Petty and Emma Young of Pan Macmillan, who patiently waited for me to write something; Hayley Yeeles of Pollinger, who kept on telling me I could do it; Gwen Davies, Kirsty Price and Becky MacNaughton, who all read stuff for me when I'd forgotten how to think; Lynda Jones, who generously provided me with a writer's retreat when I needed one, and Graham Tomlinson, who, as always, was patient, helpful and utterly brilliant.

And thanks once again to Paston College, Norfolk, for keeping me attached to the real world. ☺

But most of all, this book owes a great big debt of thanks to Dolly Parton – a true living legend – and to three other inspirational stars who are twinkling in the sky: Johnny Cash, Jim Morrison and River Phoenix.

Shine on.

Have a chat with Hayley at **f**/HayleyLongAuthor
and find out more at mykindabook.com/hayleylong